WINTER RETURN

WINTER RETURN

John Espey

JOHN DANIEL & COMPANY
PUBLISHERS
Santa Barbara / 1992

Chapter 1, in a different form, first appeared in *Crosscurrents*.

Design and typography by Jim Cook

Published by John Daniel and Company, a division of
Daniel and Daniel, Publishers, Inc., Post Office Box 21922,
Santa Barbara, California 93121. Distributed by National Book
Network, 4720 Boston Way, Lanham, Maryland 20706

LIBRARY OF CONGRESS CATALOGING-IN-PUBLICATION DATA
Espey, John Jenkins, 1913–
    Winter return / John Espey.
        p.   cm.
    ISBN 0-936784-97-0
    I. Title.
PS3509.S537W56   1992   91-47953
813'.54—dc20   CIP

For Susan and Alice

"NOW, PAPA . . . " my mother began, looking directly at me, and I waited for her to reach my name as she called the roll of the men in her life. "Now, Papa—I mean Drew . . . " and I thought of her only brother. "Now, Papa—Drew—I mean Gordon . . . " but she kept her eyes on me, not even glancing at my father, the Rev. Thomas Gordon Jerome, who sat across the room, his right hand gripping his crutches. That her father had been dead since 1921, her brother since 1933, meant nothing even now in 1950. If you had lined them up beside Father, though, you would have caught the resemblance, mostly facial; for Father was shorter and more compactly muscled than either my grandfather or my uncle had been.

"Now, Papa—Drew—Gordon—I mean *Tom,*" she said. We were home at last.

"Yes, Mother?"

"Tom, I want you to remember not to sign over the mineral rights if any other heir objects. I can't believe—I've never believed—that Papa held that acreage just to own some grazing land in Wyoming."

"Well, perhaps not," I said. We had gone over this endlessly.

"You must remember," she said, "that your Grandfather Lloyd understood such things, which I'm afraid you never have."

"I suppose not," I said, getting up. "Anyway, I'd better start. I'd like to cross the desert by afternoon, and if I'm not sleepy I'll keep on driving until I feel like stopping. Then when I get up tomorrow morning I'll just carry on. I might make it to the Knellers' place in Wyoming by the second night."

"You must drive carefully, Tom," Father said. "You've never been practical, and now in the winter you may hit snow. I hope you have an adequate map."

"Yes," I said, pulling a folded sheet from the breast pocket of my herring-bone tweed jacket. Father enjoyed maps, might even, as an ordained Presbyterian minister and sometime missionary to China, be said to believe in maps. As I opened this one he reached out for it. I had traced my route from California to Wyoming and on to Iowa with a marking pen. The blue lines looked like the veins on the back of Father's hands, especially where I had marked possible variants.

"Good," he said. "I suppose the Auto Club planned this for you?"

"As a matter of fact, no," I answered. "I just picked what looked like the most interesting roads without taking me too far out of the main way."

Father frowned. "The Club would have been happy to indicate the *best* roads, especially for this season." He handed back the map and began to arrange his crutches.

"Don't worry," I said. "I've even got chains in the trunk."

"I do hope you will be—*circumspect,* shall I say?—when you talk to Mr. Kneller," Mother said as we both looked away from Father struggling up from his chair and balancing. "If you can, Tom, sound him out."

"I'll try."

"I suppose Netty's right, and we ought to settle the whole thing now, especially after she has checked it so carefully—at least according to her."

"I'll see what I can find out," I said as we moved to the front door.

"It's just that if you had *known* your Grandfather Lloyd," she said in a tone that implied I was somehow at fault.

"Yes, Mother."

"You have the power-of-attorney?"

"In my briefcase with the other papers."

I reached the door with a sense of fading ritual. A member of the family was setting forth on a journey, and even if it came to a matter of no more than a couple of weeks, it meant a parting. At least they no longer insisted on a prayer, though that did not mean they thought their only son, now thirty-seven, stood in any less need of one than in the days when he started off to boarding school after a holiday.

"It's generous of Amy and the girls to let you go alone," Mother said.

"Amy thinks I need a rest, or at least a change," I said, "and you know how I enjoy driving." I was not going to repeat everything Amy had said about my state of mind and what she trusted this trip would do for me. Even my sister Fran, three years my elder, had called me from San Francisco, urging me to go.

"Sometimes it's useful to be alone," Father said. "You can think things over undisturbed."

"Yes," I said, relaxing myself for what was coming.

"For example," he went on, "you will be able to reflect on yourself in relation to your *profession.*"

"Yes, Father."

He cleared his throat. I waited. He rarely went further than this. I had been dedicated in infancy to the service of the Lord of the Presbyterian Church of the U.S.A. (North), and Father could never reconcile this with my being a professor of English. Thus his stress on "profession." In his hierarchy of values all eternity and the better part of salvation separated "profession" from "calling."

That Father himself had never been able to change, that he had steadfastly shattered himself upon the Calvinism of his youth could not be spoken.

He moved ahead.

Mother and I followed him out to the driveway of their house on Elizabeth Street in Pasadena. "Your Grandfather Lloyd was a great driver," Mother said. "He owned one of the first cars in the north of Iowa, you know. And your Uncle Drew was a splendid driver— your cousin Brooks, too, poor boy. And you do remember the tours we took—the four of us—when we came home on furlough?"

"I remember them."

"Be sure to give my love to Martha when you get to Dalton," she said, "and her husband, too. I keep forgetting his name."

"Bert," I said, "Bert Kratz."

"Of course."

We kissed. I patted Father on his right shoulder. Then I got behind the wheel of the Chevy, turned on the motor, warmed it up as Father nodded approvingly, and started off, not failing to wave as I entered Elizabeth Street and turned east.

Forget those tours? My right hand would lose what cunning it had and my tongue would cleave to my mouth. Those tours had reshaped, made firm, my vision of the promised land first born in my mind in Shanghai whenever my parents spoke of "home"—of what things were like "at home," what food, tasting like manna, they ate "at home"—the measureless superiority of everything in that other, that true, Jerusalem over what we experienced by the rivers of China.

And though the actuality when I entered it that summer—I was almost nine—that summer spent in Dalton, Iowa, up in the north of the state—may not have corresponded exactly with that first innocent vision, the vision itself had never completely dimmed. When, two years later, the time came to go back to Shanghai, Father bought the chassis of a Model T Ford that had lost its body in a garage fire at Chautauqua, New York, and rebuilt it in the front yard of his widowed mother's summer cottage. Once it was drivable he cruised up to Buffalo, using an orange crate for a seat, and came back in triumph with a new black four-door sedan Body by Fisher.

We drove across the continent, and as we drove my vision renewed itself. During the earlier stages of our crossing we rarely camped more than one night anywhere, unless it was Sunday. Quivering at our top speed of forty-five miles an hour over the body of the land, I knew a yearning and a delight that I have never quite lost, a yearning after and a love for the small towns with their swimming pools, the young people lounging about them, the distant notes of their laughter calling to me as we churned past—the lakes dotted with brightly colored canoes—the lights coming on at dusk.

As we made our way in the heat through that heartland my heart throbbed in response.

Oh yes, I remembered those tours. That one and the one seven years later in the Model A—for we moved with the times—when instead of camping we stopped at lodgings in the east and cabins in the west. And still, though my vision had been altered, I felt the secret life of the land beating just out of reach. More than once, at the sight of a stand of trees, a lake, a laughing group coming out of a roadhouse, a party under the glow of Japanese lanterns, I wanted to call out, to say, "Stop! Here's where I'm getting off. Goodbye!"

I couldn't, of course. I was on my way to college in Los Angeles then. Mother and Father and Fran, who had just graduated from college, were going back to China. That was the year I met Rick Bedloe, whose mother's family had lived in Pasadena since the sixth day of the Creation. Rick and I were roommates, and that Thanksgiving the Bedloes invited me over for the weekend and I met Rick's boyhood friends, Gary Frazier and David Mendl. I thought of them now. For a short time we had been a real foursome, playing our private variation of tennis. We called it "Leaf Out" because the Fraziers' court was bordered on one side by a couple of sycamore trees that dropped their leaves on it. In the beginning if a player hit a leaf he had the choice of repeating the point or saving his "leaf out" for later. Later, with the leaves in fixed positions, we created an elaborate set of random rules and "leaf out" took on a meaning of its own.

From time to time Rick tried to get together with Gary and me as if it still meant something. Rick was great, but a bit dense. How could we hope to revive the past when whatever was left of David, killed in the Second World War, lay in a North African grave?

I remembered how each of us had once spoken of what it meant to start a journey. For me, it's a precise situation that makes the real beginning of a trip. I have to be rolling in the car with no more stops to make until I want to make one. On those family tours we never got off to a simple start. The car would be loaded and we would all get in, only to find that Father had to pick up something at a drug store or Mother wanted to hunt out an early opening market. Or we would have to pull into a filling station as soon as we hit one because Father hadn't stopped for gas the night before.

During these delays I sat on the back seat beside Fran in an agony of tension while the world, the secret world calling me, waited.

This time I had had the Chevy's tank filled the night before, and I had said goodbye to Amy and the girls, Maude and Mary, and driven across the city to Pasadena, where I made my one inescapable overnight stop. So I was truly started now—I was on my way—I was on my way to Dalton. I flicked the radio switch and tuned to a popular music program.

I never call Dalton, Iowa, my home town, because I was born in Shanghai, but Dalton is the closest thing I have to an American home town, and I couldn't help thinking how just it was that I was going there both to meet the past and to settle it.

Grandfather Lloyd's estate would finally be closed. We had heard of his death a few months before we got to Dalton that first summer of my American memories. His estate had not been closed before this because, like Mother, Grandfather Lloyd's other children—my Uncle Drew, now dead, their sister Louise, and their surviving half-sister, Netty—wanted to keep a share of the mineral rights in the Wyoming acreage, whereas Mr. Kneller, who had leased the land for years, and whose property adjoined—even, I gathered, came close to surrounding Grandfather Lloyd's—insisted that he wanted clear title to everything.

Mr. Kneller complicated things by insisting that the mineral rights were worthless, that it was just a piece of pretty good grazing land in west central Wyoming, thus convincing the heirs that there must be oil there to make him so stubborn, or a vein of gold, or at the very least silver or mercury, or something else that would prove of great price.

All my life I had heard of the Wyoming acreage, and when I was a boy I, too, had visions of untold wealth pouring forth from it, and I could believe that Mr. Kneller was hiding the fact that he had made a rich strike while sinking a post hole.

"Or coal," someone said once. "There's coal in Wyoming, you know." Even if that took the glamour out of it, it still offered something solid.

I can't remember just when I began to lose my innocence, to suspect this vision, but by now I thought only of how typical, how perfectly correct it was for an American family of some generations' standing and no particular distinction to hold this dream property "out west."

Driving east through the towns of the San Gabriel Valley, I smiled at the faith that Grandfather Lloyd's children still put in his judgment. When Amy and I, having paid off our Depression debts, bought our first house, we upset my parents badly because we hadn't consulted them. But finally Mother said, "Well, Papa—Drew—Gordon—I mean *Tom,* even if you didn't *know* it, you were doing a wise thing. Papa always said that real estate in a growing community guarantees a sound investment." She said this as if Grandfather Lloyd alone among men had received this wisdom from on high and that it was an item of private lore to be cherished and handed down secretly in the family.

"I'm certainly happy to learn that," I said, and Mother, normally alert to tone, failed to catch the irony.

Even on matters that I found it increasingly hard to believe that Grandfather Lloyd had had the slightest competence in, his views were cited. I felt it unjust that I, as the rightful inheritor, was not credited with grasping any of this knowledge. I was a scrawny, sickly kid, and I suspected that both Mother and Father wondered at times how the glorious line of "Papa-Drew-Gordon" could have ended in this rickety, asthmatic "I mean *Tom.*"

About the time I felt my first doubts about Grandfather Lloyd I sensed that Mother sometimes hesitated, breaking her normal rhythm after she reached me in her recital, as if she might go on. I was about six, maybe seven, when I learned that she had been delivered of a stillborn infant when I was two years old, and Fran five. Whenever I had shown myself completely unworthy and was being quoted some bit of Grandfather Lloyd's wisdom I was haunted by this ghostly little brother—for the small body was a boy's—this sturdy lad whose name would have been Gordon, "beautifully, perfectly formed" they would say when they spoke of him. He would have been everything the line deserved. Had he lived he would surely have spared me many a burden. From time to time I thought of him with hate and envy and longing and—yes—even with love.

Grandfather Lloyd's quoted pronouncements extended to the smallest matters. When I drove over to Pasadena one afternoon I saw Father at the end of the back yard, jabbing at the ground with one of his crutches as he supported himself with the other.

"What's the trouble?" I called as I hurried toward him.

"I'm killing this spider."

"Oh, a black widow!" I exclaimed. "Here, I'll take care of it."

Then I saw it wasn't a black widow but a large gold garden spider. "It's harmless, Father. You needn't worry about it."

But he had already maimed it, so I stepped on it to stop its crippled, indrawn writhing. As I did this, Father said, "Tom, if you kill *all* spiders you don't need to worry over which are poisonous and which not."

"That doesn't make sense, Father," I said, looking at the smeared grass. "The one poisonous spider in this part of California is the black widow. It's easy to spot and so is its web. Once you know that you can leave the harmless ones alone."

"Tom," Father said, "when I first went to Iowa to meet your mother's family, your Grandfather Lloyd told me it was wise to kill all spiders. If you do that, he said, you don't have to worry about which are poisonous and which not. Your Grandfather Lloyd was a wise man."

"But really . . . " I began, and stopped. Father's voice had betrayed an all too familiar irritation and disappointment. I turned to something else, something meaningless and neutral, like the new Detroit models, as we moved slowly to the back door.

What made a little independence possible for me was my discovery quite early that I had two minds, if not two bodies.

Without being pretentious about it, it began with the simple act of drinking tea.

In the front of the three-story brick house there in the Presbyterian Mission compound in Shanghai everyone knew—I suspected that Grandfather Lloyd had issued a proclamation on the subject—that for a child to drink tea of any strength would stunt his growth and wreak havoc with his mental development, and when I was in the front of the house I never doubted this. But in the back of the house, when I sat at the square table in the middle of the kitchen with our servants, it was well known that nothing could be more stimulating to the mind and a better protection from most sicknesses than swig after swig of strong green tea sucked from the spout of the communal pot as it passed from hand to hand.

The first real thinking I did was to separate these worlds, never to be confused. I did not drink a cup of strong tea in the front of the house until I was sixteen and had grown to be a trifle over six feet tall, an attenuated, skeletal sixteen-year-old, but certainly not a stunted one. Even so, I felt myself repeatedly torn as I grew older, caught between my own two minds and a more public mind that I came to think of as Grandfather Lloyd's.

Shortly after I met Amy in college I knew that we would marry. One Thursday afternoon as we walked across the campus to the library I told her I had to decide whether to spend the weekend— she was going to the beach with her mother—finishing a paper on *The Road to Xanadu* or in Pasadena, where I had been invited to stay overnight and go to the Valley Hunt Club to play tennis by the Dickeys, boyhood friends of Father's.

"What's the problem?" Amy asked. "Why don't you just do whichever you'd rather?"

Hearing her ask this as if it were a possible way of living one's life shook me. That was when I knew we would marry. It was an instant thing, but it was not at all my idea of falling in love. I had fallen in love time and time again, from kindergarten on, and at first, second, and third sight. But this was different. Just as I knew that I was going to the Dickeys', I knew this other decision was final too.

I was approaching the outskirts of San Bernardino by now and passed by citrus groves and vineyards. That way of life was dying, subdivisions beginning to spread out from each town, and I thought of how much the area had changed from my first memory of it, when we were on our way back to China the summer following that first summer in Dalton. I had come a long way, even if I was just starting this particular trip.

Our trip to America that long ago summer started under a shadow. We had looked forward to it for almost a year, and then late one Friday afternoon in April Father came for Fran and me at the Shanghai American School. He sometimes came for us in our Chevrolet Baby Grand touring car, but that afternoon I knew the car was in the garage for repairs and that something special must have happened, because Fran and I were used to taking the streetcar ride home by ourselves.

For a long time Father sat between us, silent, and as the tram clanged down North Szechuan Road I fell into a trance, lulled by the rocking car. When I came out of it I stared at Father's left hand as it rested on his knee beside me. Focusing carefully, I refused to let my eyes leave it, trying to make certain that it really was Father sitting beside me. I stared at the veins, trying to remember their exact pattern, not daring to lift my eyes for fear that the man beside me would not be Father and that I had been abandoned.

But this game of Lost in the Big City was no good this afternoon. I was too old to worry about finding myself alone in Shanghai, and no matter how hard I looked at Father's hand, I couldn't help seeing a few square inches of Fran's pleated tartan skirt beyond it.

We were leaving the International Settlement and entering Frenchtown, so I shifted to playing Hate the Kaiser. One of my greatest regrets was that the war had ended before I could play my destined part in Flanders Fields, but here in Shanghai, at least, we had clung for a time to a spirit of Gallic vengeance that kept the war alive. With the Armistice signed, the French government of Shanghai declared all Germans *personae non gratae* in their Concession. Any German wishing to go from the International Settlement to Chinese territory, where we lived, had to get off the streetcar and hire a sampan to take him upriver unless the German was willing to risk a ride straight through and be subject to arrest and a heavy fine.

My role here was not the usually appealing one of fugitive, the loner risking all. No, I was the astute detective who smelled out the Teutonism of the invader and denounced him to the authorities, thus earning glory and possibly a material reward. I penetrated the most elaborate ruses. I dealt ruthlessly with women who disguised themselves as nuns accompanying young children. No matter how my victims humbled themselves before me I could not be moved to pity. "You have served the Kaiser and the Kaiserin," I declared harshly. "You must pay."

Father interrupted my gloating as he cleared his throat and said, "Children, I came for you so that I could tell you something painful before we get home. You must be ready to find your mother badly upset. Word came this morning by cable after you had left for school that your Grandfather Lloyd has died suddenly."

No one spoke for perhaps a minute as the car rocked along to its next stop, the motorman clanging his foot bell to scatter the rickshaws and carts ahead of us.

At last I said, "Then we won't see him when we get to Dalton this summer."

"No, you won't, Tom," Father said. "The important thing now is to remember that your mother is very sad. She still hasn't got over the news last month about your Aunt Floss, so this comes as an extra heavy shock."

"Aunt Floss died having a baby, didn't she?" I asked.

"Yes, she was in a hospital and they couldn't save her. She kept calling for her father—your Grandfather Lloyd—to come. I think that was what made your mother especially unhappy. The baby is with your Grandma Tessy and Aunt Netty now in Dalton."

"Actually, Tom," Fran said, "Aunt Floss was Mother's half-sister, just like Aunt Netty. She was a *half*-aunt, like Aunt Netty. Her mother is Grandma Tessy, not Grandmother Lloyd, who was *our* grandmother. *Our* grandmother died when Mother was twelve years old."

"I know all that. But you wouldn't want me to call her *Half*-Aunt Floss, would you?"

"I don't think that is very funny, Tom," Fran said.

"Your mother may be resting when we get home," Father said as if he had heard neither of us. "I think the best thing is just to go in and kiss her, and then if she doesn't seem to want you to stay, or if she is crying, you mustn't feel hurt. Grandfather Lloyd meant a great deal to her, naturally, and she had been so looking forward to seeing him again after all these years."

"Now I won't see either of my grandfathers to remember them," I said, because our Grandfather Jerome had died five years before.

"Him," Father said.

"What?" I asked.

"Him," he repeated. " 'Either one of my grandfathers to remember *him*' would be the full construction."

"Yes, Father," I said, miffed.

"I shall remember them from having seen them both," Fran said, "and I shall be happy to describe either or both of them to you at any time you wish, Tom."

"I don't need to have them described to me," I said. "I've seen their pictures in the albums, their pictures taken with *me.* I *know* what they looked like. I just won't have seen them to remember."

"That's what I mean," Fran said. "I *have* seen them to remember. It's just that you were too *young.* You were only eighteen months old when we came back from America that time."

"I know that," I said, "and that isn't what I meant, thank you very much."

"There's no reason to be rude about it."

"I'm not being rude," I said and measured the distance to see if I could kick her in the shin without kicking Father as well.

"If you kick me, Tom, I'll never, never tell you another thing about either of our grandfathers."

Father came to at this. "Children! Have you already forgotten that your Grandfather Lloyd has just died?"

I had forgotten, and it was a relief to forget, but now I felt guilty. We sat silent as the streetcar ground on past the godowns on the French Bund. At the end of the line we got off and walked through Fish Market Street to the old East Gate, where we took another car to the Little South Gate. We got off and walked through Mulberry Lane to our compound.

Mother lay on the guest-room bed under a steamer rug. Fran bent over, kissed her cheek, and stood back. It was my turn. As I kissed Mother she began to sob. Anger took hold of me and I said, "Why are you crying for *him?* I'm as good as he was."

Mother stopped sobbing and looked up at me. Father stared straight ahead.

"What did you say, Tom?" Mother asked.

I stood paralyzed. I could never repeat those words.

"What did you say, Tom?" she repeated.

"Answer your mother, Tom," Father said, looking at me now.

"I don't know," I lied. "I don't remember. Nothing, Mother, nothing!"

But I knew they had all heard.

"Tom," Mother said, "your Grandfather Lloyd was a wonderful man, a great man. You will be lucky to be anything like him."

"Yes, Mother."

She began sobbing again and Father gestured toward the door.

I felt lost, forsaken utterly. Fran went straight to her room and shut the door. I thought of following her to see if I could start a fight. Instead, I went down the steep servants' staircase and stepped into the kitchen.

The cook and his wife, our amah, stopped talking. Then the amah said in Chinese, "You are back from school, Little Brother," using the familiar name I was called at home.

"I am back from school," I said in Chinese.

"You have been told that your grandfather has died."

"I have been told."

"And what do you feel?" the cook asked.

"Nothing," I said. "I can't remember him. He is a picture in the picture book."

"Your mother says he was a very good, a very great man," the amah said.

"That is what she says."

I had lied when I said I felt nothing, because I felt stricken, pierced, not by Grandfather Lloyd's death, but because Mother and Father had looked at me in horror and disgust a few minutes ago.

"Can we do anything for you, Little Brother?" the cook asked.

"No, thank you," I said. "I am just going to drink some tea."

I went to the square table and sat on a stool. They returned to their work. I lifted the teapot, put the spout in my mouth and sucked on it. A curled leaf came through on the third pull. I sat there a long time, chewing its bitterness.

2

AFTER SKIRTING San Bernardino I drove up out of the San Gabriel Valley and over Cajon Pass. Looking to the east I saw the first stretches of desert as the road brought me curving down from the mountains to the flats. The Great American Desert lay before me, the desert that might or might not make you a Westerner once you had crossed it east to west. I had crossed the Great American Desert a number of times, and in both directions, before I sensed that I had become a Westerner. I remembered Amy's surprised joy a few years before this when, on a family tour, we headed back to L.A. from the East and I said, without thinking about it, "It'll be a relief to get back home where we belong. Not that I'm complaining, but . . . "

"You really mean it?"

"Sure, why would I . . . ?"

"You wouldn't accept even a *terrific* offer from the East or the Middle West?"

"Never! What makes you think . . . ?"

"Well, they don't seem to be for me, but I thought that for *you* . . . and I don't mean that the girls and I wouldn't go along if it came to . . . "

"Forget it," I said, laughing, tempted to tease her. "To tell the truth there is *one* offer I'd consider seriously."

I regretted this as soon as I heard the worried note in her query, "And what would that be?"

"Appointment as a Fellow of All Souls, Oxford, for life."

She snickered. Mary and Maude giggled behind me on the back seat. Amy turned to them and said, "How did we ever get ourselves hooked up with such a clown?"

"Anyway," I said, keeping my eye on the road, "you can forget all that. We should be singing 'California, here I come!' "

As the four of us struck into that rousing chant Amy patted my right knee and moved her hand up along my thigh and into my crotch. Fitting the words to the tune, I sang out, "Not in front of the children, dear!" and she answered with a squeeze that threatened to guarantee we could never have any more.

To this day, whenever I cross the continent from west to east I feel a sense of reversing the correct pattern—the movement of the American over the body of the land, arriving on the Eastern sea-board, then passing through the Alleghenies, followed by a long pause on the Great Plains to gather strength for crossing the Desert and the Mountains to gain the Pacific shore. How many generations should it take to get that far? And once the rim of the Pacific is reached, what's left but to make the great leap, the act of faith, across those waters? Mother and Father had made that leap, a commitment beyond my capacity, if not my understanding. Indeed, it had been almost beyond Father's capacity, leaving him crippled and forcing him to retire in his mid-fifties.

For myself, I'd never seen anything but a return to America. Not that I hadn't physically completed the great circle, crossing into Europe from China by way of the Trans-Siberian Express—was it really twelve days from Manchouli to Berlin?—with a six months' pause before making the other, the "safe" leap across the Atlantic. I had even—as if my generation had to do everything twice before discovering itself—completed the circle again, taking Their Britannic Majesties' Imperial Tour, stopping off at the blindly confident outposts of empire east of Suez. Then on up the Red Sea and through the Canal, to end in Our Old Home itself and three years up at Oxford, which yielded three meaningless degrees. Meaningless because I knew all along that I was in bondage to America, that I was an American, whatever that meant. It can be trying to find yourself an American and a Westerner when the only way you can define those labels is by negatives.

If the moral tone of my American world derived from Grandfather Lloyd's dicta, its physical quality remained equally precise. I drew that scene from the pages of popular magazines as I pored over their illustrations and ads in Shanghai. My hero modeled himself on J.C. Leyendecker's Arrow Collar man, whose features I was to recognize years later echoed in the slightly pouting mouth and gray eyes of F. Scott Fitzgerald. His pectorals put the gentlest possible strain on the smooth, striped fabric of his shirt in a way that filled my concave chest with despair. Even when handling a small boat, the Arrow Collar man looked into the middle distance, his hand casual and confident on the tiller, his green foulard necktie bent in a breeze that left his honey-colored hair unruffled.

What part could I hope to play in a world made for this handsome, self-confident young god? I saw the purely physical world courtesy of Edward Penfield and Maxfield Parrish. It shone blue-gold in the evening, the last light of day burnishing the leaves of a copper beech with rays reflected from a pool mirroring fountain jets.

In such a world even Grandfather Lloyd's absolutes might become reasonable and attractive. Certainly it was not a world where anyone would dream of swigging tea from the spout of the pot. Though disheartening, this suggested at the same time an elevation of the body, a purified sensuality offering a relationship between the Arrow Collar god and his virginal companion in middy blouse and black bandanna, that was infinitely rewarding, somehow tactile without requiring the vulgarity of touch.

Now as the road flattened I began to let the car out, forgetting for the time being all this cant of Americans and being a Westerner as I thought back to that first summer in Dalton. But before I let myself get into that trans-Pacific crossing I remembered the lifeless feeling of the weekend that followed Father's announcement of Grandfather Lloyd's death.

I can't say I was exactly put in Coventry, because Fran did speak to me from time to time, and Father tried to behave as if nothing had happened, continuing to address the Lord in his blessings before meals and at both early morning prayers in Chinese with the servants and family prayers at night. Mother left the guest room Sunday morning but did not come down for breakfast. I wanted to go in to see her and apologize, but Father told Fran and me we still shouldn't bother her.

I held to the wan hope that our collective grief should allow Fran and me to skip school at least for Monday, but we had no such luck. Mother came down to breakfast that morning, self-consciously cheerful and "normal," so I knew there was no chance. I still felt desolate, deserted, though Fran was beginning to act less like a tragic princess. The thought of school plunged me deeper into isolation, but when Mother went out to the kitchen after breakfast and Fran and I had ten minutes before we had to leave for our streetcar ride, I saw my chance to make the day bearable.

I took the stairs two at a time and went into Mother and Father's bedroom. I pulled open the bureau drawer that held Mother's jewel box. I'd learned to pick the lock with a hairpin long ago, and I did this now. Before anyone else came upstairs I took out the silver filigree necklace with the purple cat's-eyes, relocked the box and pushed the drawer back in. I could hear Fran saying something on the stairs, so I tiptoed into the nursery bathroom, slammed both doors, and locked them.

I made it just in time. As I loosened my necktie and unbuttoned my collar, Fran tried the door into the upstairs hall.

"I'll let you in in a minute," I called. "After all, I'm on the pot, you know."

"Well, try to cover the stink you're making with a decent amount of Jeyes Fluid," she said. "Anyway, I can use Mother and Father's bathroom, so don't hold back."

What a relief it was to have Fran herself again! Most of the time it was Fran and me against the world—against the Mission, against the bloodthirsty Jehovah hovering over us in a black cloud, against the namby-pamby Jesus we had to swallow every day—and even when we fought we were really both on the same side. Poor old Bible world! It didn't have a chance.

I knew that the beautiful necklace went three times round my neck. I fastened the clasp and rebuttoned my collar and rearranged my tie. Then I used the pot and the Jeyes Fluid.

Purple was my favorite color; not, alas, an anywhere near decent color for a red-blooded American boy to admire. But with that beautiful necklace, that wonderful color against my throat, I could face a day at school, face almost anything, especially since Fran had relented. Not that I had ever dared tell her what I did on my most desperate days.

But when life seemed too much to tolerate I could feel my purple talisman and rejoice in its protection. I had to be careful while I was with Fran because if I touched my shirt over the necklace too often she would ask me why I was so fidgety. And at school I lived in delight and terror, afraid that I might get involved in a friendly tussle with my Courtesy Cousin Henry Myers or a friend like Walter Hiltner or Joe McCracken that would expose my silver-and-purple secret.

Worse than that would be a bullying from a fifth-grader who sometimes picked on us, Bill Brewster. He'd never quite made up for a crazy impulse I'd had earlier that year when he stood at the top of the playground slide and wouldn't go down or let anyone pass him. In a spasm of rage I had scuttled up the ladder and given him a push in the back that sent him sprawling down head first with me coming down right behind. I had run off the playground and hidden in the shrubbery by the First through Third Grades Building while he hunted for me, shouting that he would kill me. But too many of my classmates, especially the girls, mocked him for being beaten by the skinniest kid in the whole school for him to quite admit to it by taking a delayed revenge. Still, I always kept an eye out for him.

Luckily, that Monday went smoothly enough. From time to time I put my hand around the base of my neck and knew that all was well in my hidden world.

Getting the necklace back into the jewel box involved its own risks. I had to figure out where everyone was, and sometimes I even had to wait in an agony of fear overnight, before I could put it back safely. Still, it was worth the risk. And that particular afternoon Fran wanted to finish some project of her own in her room, and I was home free before it was time for dinner.

In a few days the mood lightened. After all, Mother, Fran and I were going "home"—Father would follow us in a year on his regular furlough—and even if Grandfather Lloyd was dead, something must be left. The three of us were leaving Father for the year because Fran and I both needed to have our teeth straightened, and Shanghai, for all its wealth and variety, didn't as yet boast an orthodontist.

"No child of mine is going to go through life with a serious overbite," Mother had declared in her characteristically ironic rhetoric after my front teeth had come in at as bad an angle as Fran's. "The children will have enough to cope with when they're in college and on their own without *that* handicap."

So trunks and suitcases came down from the attic and the untidy excitement of packing filled our old nursery. Our house stood in some ways as the social center of the mission compound. Not only did Mother enjoy entertaining and Father bear the responsibility for a lot of mission affairs, but Fran and I were the only foreign children in the compound, making ours the one complete family household, frequently visited by the other members of the mission.

Fran and I got a great deal of information from these visitors about what "home" was like that spring, information that Fran accepted haughtily. I myself grew annoyed at being told time after time that I must be careful crossing streets in American cities because at "home" traffic kept to the right—"the right way," as this was usually expressed—instead of to the left—"the English way"—as in Shanghai.

One Saturday morning a young member of the mission, the Rev. Joseph Hamilton Carter, who thought himself something of a wit, stopped by to consult Father on a point of mission policy. Father wasn't in, but Mr. Carter—he was too young to be considered a Courtesy Uncle—caught sight of me in the downstairs hall and said, "Ah, Tom, even if your revered and reverend father isn't here, my call won't go unspent. I had a little change left over when I came back from home last summer, and I thought I would give it to you for a going-away present."

He pulled out some coins from a jacket pocket and dropped them into my hand. I had seen enough American money to recognize three quarters, two dimes, and four pennies.

"Oh, thank you very much, Mr. Carter," I said.

"You're quite welcome," he said. "Be sure to spend it wisely."

"Yes, Mr. Carter."

Then, in what I recognized as his pulpit voice he recited: " 'For the good man is not at home, he is gone a long journey: He hath taken a bag of money with him, and will come home at the day appointed.' "

"That must be from the Bible," I said as politely as I could, trying not to laugh at his silly voice.

"You are a shrewd young man," Mr. Carter said. "Proverbs, Chapter Seven, verses 19 and 20."

"Yes, sir," I said. "I knew it sounded familiar."

He paused at the front door, hand in pocket. "There ought to be one more coin," he said. "Aha, here it is, a *gen-you-wine* plug nickel for a luck piece. Catch!"

He tossed the dull bit of metal in a high parabola and it stung my palm as I caught it.

"Thank you very much again, sir," I said.

"Don't mention it," Mr. Carter said, chuckling as he shut the front door behind him.

In the nursery, Mother bent over a steamer trunk. "Mr. Carter gave me some American coins he had left over," I said.

"That's nice," she said, going on packing. "I hope you thanked him."

"Of course."

"That's all right then," she said. "Tom, I'm really very busy right now."

"Yes, Mother," I said, thinking I needn't mention the money again.

Before tea that afternoon I asked Fran, "What would a *plug* nickel be?"

"That would be a bad one, one that wasn't a real one," she informed me loftily.

"You mean like a bad Chinese twenty-cent piece that doesn't ring true and is worth less than a good one?"

"Not exactly," she said. "Those bad twenty-cent pieces do have *some* silver in them. That's why you can still use them even if you get fewer coppers than for the others. But with an American piece of money it's either all good or all bad."

"You mean it would be cheating to spend it?"

"Naturally," she said, "and dangerous too. You could be arrested and put in jail."

I wasn't sure Mr. Carter had done me any great favor giving me a piece of money that might land me in jail. He had said it could be a good luck piece, but I wondered. Still, there was always the good money.

Just before family prayers the next night I spoke to Father alone in his study. "Fran says a plug piece of American money is a bad piece of money."

"That's true," he said.

"Then it would be a kind of sin to spend it even if you could?"

"Well, it certainly wouldn't be *right*."

I kept my American money far back on my closet shelf. Fran and I had each been given a small suitcase for our personal things. The day before we sailed I tied up the coins in a handkerchief, tucking it into a rolled pair of black knee-length stockings.

I bowed my head impatiently there in our first-class cabin on the *Empress of Asia* after we had boarded her from the tender taking us down the Whangpoo and into the mouth of the Yangtze. I was so used to being prayed over that I paid little attention to Father's demands for guidance and protection, not to mention the instructions to his children as to how to behave that somehow worked their way into his one-sided exchange with the Lord. The warning gong for visitors brought him to a hurried close, and after we had waved and waved until the tender disappeared we felt the throb of the liner's engines under our feet. At last the anchor came up. We heeled over, heading for the open sea.

After coaling at Nagasaki and a day's tour of Yokohama we left the Japanese Toyland behind. The days at sea stretched out luxuriously as I drove on in my home-going dream. A few days out of Vancouver I came down with a crashing attack of asthma, the bane of my life. Even so, I felt prepared to enter into the promised land, where all troubles would surely cease, possibly even asthma.

As we waited in the first-class saloon for passport inspection, an unusual quaver in Mother's voice brought me out of myself. I had never known her daunted before. "Children," she said, "let us have a few moments of silent prayer to help us through these trials and the trials that lie before us." Why was she sounding so much like the Scriptures?

Mother closed her eyes and bowed her head. Fran bowed her head, but I wasn't sure that she didn't peek to the side. Why we had anything to fear now that we had crossed the Pacific I couldn't imagine. Cosmopolitan enough to be embarrassed by the scene we made, I kept my head up, my eyes half-open, squinting angrily at anyone who dared look at us for more than an instant.

Mother's appeal ended, we were taken care of by the Customs service and the Canadian Pacific Railway with such efficiency and dispatch that I could see Mother felt her prayer had been answered. I couldn't help thinking that this service had been performed many times for many persons. Still, I wasn't going to raise this theological issue, and we were soon out of it all anyway.

The next day we swung along in a sleeping car through the Canadian Rockies. The mountains rose magnificently and we still weren't even "home" truly, because Canada was, after all, just a slice of the British Empire. Once I refused to obey a warning call and stayed in the open-air observation car through a long tunnel. Though I came out with face and clothes sooty, my asthma had lifted a little.

Uncle Carl, Aunt Netty's husband, met us in Minneapolis and installed us overnight in a hotel. Grandma Tessy called us long distance, and after talking with Mother for a few minutes she must have asked to speak to Fran and me.

Fran kept up a glibly polite exchange.

I already suffered from a telephone phobia among my other inadequacies. When my turn came I couldn't think of anything to say after I had announced, "This is Tom."

Grandma Tessy's trace of southern accent made her sound foreign, though I understood her perfectly when she asked if I wasn't happy to be home in America at last. I didn't know why I couldn't say anything sensible, but each time she tried to get an answer out of me I bleated "I beg your pardon?" hoping everyone would think I hadn't heard her clearly.

Fran looked at me with contempt. Finally Mother took the receiver and said, "I'm afraid Tom is tongue-tied for the first time in his life!"

I could hear a sound that I would think of later as Grandma Tessy's southern-belle laughter.

"Couldn't you think of *anything* to say, Tom?" Mother asked as she hung up. "You usually say too much, you know."

"She talks in a funny way."

"Oh, come on," Mother said, smiling. "You've heard plenty of southerners in Shanghai. I've even heard you mimic them. It's true that Tessy holds on to that accent, but after all, she was born a Burr, a Burr of Virginia, you know."

"That sounds funny, too," I said. "I'm glad I'm not a Burr of Virginia or any other kind of sticky old burr."

Fran giggled.

"It's a good thing you didn't say that to Tessy," Mother said, unable to suppress a smile. "The Burrs of Virginia are an important family, an aristocratic family." Then she added without any special emphasis, "At least that is something they keep repeating."

"Yes!" Fran declaimed. "Their plantations were pillaged and they had no place to lay their heads at the close of the Civil War!"

"Goodness!" Mother exclaimed. "Wherever did you hear all that?"

Fran smiled. "I suppose I read it somewhere. But I really do remember somebody talking about plantations seven years ago."

"I'm not surprised," Mother said. "But, Tom, if you should ever have to talk about the Civil War with your Grandma Tessy—though

I don't know why you should—be sure to call it the War Between the States."

"Why?"

"It's considered tactful."

"You do know what the Civil War was, Tom, don't you?" Fran asked severely.

"Of course," I said, glad for a chance to be perverse. "The Civil War was fought during the second half of the seventeenth century between the Royalists under the Stuart kings and the Puritan Roundheads led by Oliver Cromwell, who became Lord Protector of England." I stuck out my tongue at the end of this recitation, and saw Fran getting a good grip on a pillow.

"Oh, don't be a complete idiot, Tom!" Fran said. "We don't mean *that* Civil War."

"I know you don't," I answered, "and ha-ha to you, sweet maid."

I got ready to dodge, but before Fran could hoist the pillow Mother said "Children!" Fran dropped the pillow and turned away, affecting to be interested in something she saw from the window.

Mother started again. "What I wanted to say, Tom, was not so much about the War Between the States as about all our Burr relatives by marriage in Dalton. I don't know quite how to put it. It isn't that they may seem unfriendly, because they are proud of being southerners and having polished manners even if they run their farms almost exactly the way everyone else does. But they may be a little—well, *distant* at times, if you know what that means."

"Even Grandma Tessy?" I asked, not being sure what Mother meant.

"No, hardly. After all, she is a Lloyd by marriage, so she tends to be on that side of it."

"Side of what?" I demanded, completely at sea.

"I guess," Mother said, "that I must tell you something, Tom, that you haven't been told up to now."

Fran wheeled around at this. I waited.

"You know that your Grandfather Lloyd was a banker," Mother began.

"Yes," I said. "He was the president of the Dalton Commercial

Bank, and Uncle Drew is vice president, and Uncle Fred is treasurer."

"That's right," Mother said, "but maybe it's best to say *was* or *were*."

"What does that mean?"

"It means your Grandfather Lloyd was a very generous man. If he had one fault that would have been it. The bank is in trouble. It looks now as if the bank—and the family—can pay back everyone's money, but it will take some time. Until that happens the bank is closed. The Burrs, like everyone else in and around Dalton, had money in the bank, and just because they are related to us by marriage they may be more upset than some of the other people."

"You mean the bank is *busted*?" I asked, incredulous.

"That's the common way of putting it, though I don't know where you would have picked that up."

"Banks in China are always going bust," I said.

"That's true, but the Dalton bank hasn't really *failed*, or gone *bankrupt*. It is just going to take some time to turn the land the bank owns into money. And we are going to have to turn some of our own family's property into money to pay off what the bank owes to people."

For some reason Fran had shrugged in the middle of this and turned back to the window.

"If it wasn't Grandfather Lloyd's fault I don't see why they should blame the rest of us," I protested.

"Certainly it wasn't his fault," Mother said quickly. "If it was anybody's fault it was . . . " She stopped herself. I waited, and she went on after a pause, "Anyway, it is something the family must take care of for its own good name."

"Aren't the Lloyds from the South, too?"

"Oh, you couldn't call Maryland quite the South, certainly not like Virginia. The Lloyds were split by the war, the Civil War, the War Between the States. That was why your grandfather left as soon as he could. He said he hated all the bickering he heard, and his step-mother didn't like him. The Lloyds were ordinary small farmers, you know—no plantations or slaves or anything like that. When your grandfather was about twenty he just bundled up his one good suit of clothes and said goodbye."

"It sounds exciting, romantic, doesn't it?" Fran said, turning back to us.

"He said the excitement lasted until his money ran out," Mother said, laughing. "At least it took him as far as Illinois and later to Iowa."

"*Our* Grandmother Lloyd wasn't from the South at all," Fran said emphatically.

"No, my mother was from New England." Mother looked across the room away from us. "The thing I remember best about her was the color of her eyes. She had violet eyes."

"They would have made her very beautiful," I said.

Neither of them seemed to hear me. Fran turned to Mother and asked, "Which side would you have been on in the Civil War?"

"The North, I suppose," Mother said automatically.

"I'd have freed the slaves right off," I said. "The Burrs must have had tons of slaves with all those plantations."

"Pillared plantation houses," Fran recited dreamily.

"I wouldn't bring it up with Tessy," Mother said, "or any of the Burrs, for that matter."

"Did Grandfather Lloyd call it the War Between the States?" I asked.

"Come to think of it," Mother said, "he never did."

"Then it can't be right, can it?" I asked.

"Oh, Tom, just try not to make any trouble!" Mother said, her eyes filling with tears.

"I'll try, really I will," I promised hastily.

The one passenger train scheduled to stop at Dalton on request left St. Paul in the early afternoon. The landscape had disappointed me as we had slanted across the Portal in North Dakota. Then after we had come into Minnesota at Fargo it had begun to pick up a good bit. Now, as we pulled out of the city into the countryside it began changing again. The small lakes, so inviting with their diving platforms and splashes of pure color, gave way to what I knew were corn fields. They stretched out to a southern eternity.

I felt the lack of decoration. The land needed something like pagodas, the pagodas that were like exclamation marks in China. Then I began to see—and it was my first feeling of beginning to know my own country—"home"—that there *were* pagodas, in two sizes. There were town pagodas by the railroad stations and farm pagodas by farmhouses.

Mother and Fran had settled into the seat across from me, and we all rocked and swayed with the hypnotizing rhythm of the train.

As we slowed down approaching a stop I pointed to a cluster of farm buildings and asked, "What's that tall round building?"

Mother said, "Why, that's called a silo. It's for storing winter fodder."

"And when they clean one out it stinks at the bottom," Fran contributed learnedly.

"And what are those two buildings across the tracks here?" We had stopped by now.

"Grain elevators," Mother said. "The farmers bring in their grain and corn to the elevator, where it's weighed and stored until it's sold and shipped out. That's why they're always beside the tracks, usually on a siding."

"Then they don't have anything to do with religion or God at all?"

"Religion!" Fran exclaimed. "How could they have anything to do with *religion?*"

"I don't know," I said, trying to retreat, because I could see that I'd blundered.

"Even if it doesn't make sense, you must have meant *something*," Fran insisted.

"Yes, Tom," Mother said. "Do tell us."

"I got to thinking that the siloes—is that right?—and the elevators are like pagodas."

"Pagodas?" Fran's voice shot up so high and shrill that Mother looked at her, shaking her head. "Pagodas?" Fran repeated in a lower voice.

"They come so regularly," I said, feeling foolish now, "and they are the only kind of real decoration around."

"But can't you see that church?" Fran asked, pointing to a meek white frame structure near the center of the small town we were now moving out of.

"Of course I've seen the churches," I said. "They just look like big wood houses. They don't do anything different."

"No, perhaps not," Mother said, but her voice broke.

"Pagodas!" Fran said and they both sputtered into laughter. I stared sourly out the window, waiting to spot the next silo. As it came into view Fran pointed at it and they were off again.

"If you can't see the difference," I said, "you might as well laugh." I wanted to add something like "you blind females," but I knew I couldn't, and anyway I wasn't sure that Father would have understood me any better.

So while they tried to control themselves I looked at the land, taking in the fields of corn, endless corn, and here and there the small islands of buildings with a few trees, and then a town, and always the two kinds of American pagoda.

I sank so deeply into this that I failed to hear what Mother was saying to me.

"I beg your pardon, Mother?"

"I said that at least you've given us a good laugh, Tom." She wiped her eyes. "I think that was something we all needed."

"I'm sure you've very welcome," I said, proud of myself for not asking where the "all" came in.

If this was the promised land I'd been misinformed.

We began slowing down for a bigger place than any we'd been through for a long time. Here and there a light showed as dusk fell.

"This is Center City, the county seat," Mother said. "Dalton comes next, but we'll stop here for five or ten minutes." Her voice changed as she went on, sounding really nervous, "Now remember, both of you, that there may be several people to meet us, your Uncle Drew, of course, and probably your cousins Brooks and Rob, but perhaps none of the Burrs, certainly not Grandma Tessy."

"Please don't worry, Mother," Fran said. "We'll be fine."

Sitting there in Center City waiting, I felt the vision begin to reassemble, taking in all the changes. More lights came on outside. The harsh outlines blurred. The heat lifted a little. When we started with a slight jerk and began rolling out of the station I could see the streets and the colored signs and lights and a cluster of older boys on one corner. So I knew the old truth was still there, hidden, disguised, as the city fell away behind us. For a moment I could see lights in a farmhouse and the finger of a silo against the darkening sky.

The lights in the coach snapped on. There sat Mother and Fran across from me, too sharp against the dusty plush, pushing back the vision as the windows now reflected each other. But I knew the other magic was still out there. At least I had learned enough to hold it private and keep my mouth shut.

The conductor came through and stopped beside us. "Well, lady, I guess we're about to Dalton," he announced.

"Yes, thank you very much," Mother said. "You're sure our luggage will be dropped off?"

"Oh sure," he said. "We still get two or three calls a week to stop at Dalton. We used to stop regular, but things have been slowing down, and with the bank . . . "

"Yes, yes," Mother interrupted as the train slowed.

I shaded my eyes, trying to see Dalton. But Fran was pulling my arm, saying, "Come *on,* Tom. You know the train just barely stops. You wouldn't want to be left behind, would you?"

"I don't know," I said, following her down the aisle, wondering what it would be like to be carried off alone to wherever the tracks might take me.

The brakes took hold, and I grabbed the back of a seat. The conductor opened the door at the end of the car and jumped down with his little platform. He helped Mother and Fran down the steps. I scrambled along behind and stepped out into the new world of Dalton.

I no longer believed now that everyone in Dalton actually came to the station that evening to welcome us as descendants of Grandfather Lloyd, but in memory at least I saw them all, saw them in three shallow concentric arcs as we stepped off the train. The arcs seemed to hold still for an instant, with the Lloyds in the first rank, the Burrs a step or two back, and behind them the people from the town.

Grandma Tessy wasn't there, and there couldn't have been enough Burrs to fill out that second arc. And probably only a few townsfolk had come to check the last mail of the day or see that their own letters made the late train. Still, there they were in my remembering eyes.

The pattern broke as Mother stepped between me and a man moving forward from the first arc. I recognized Uncle Drew from the pictures in the album. As the others waited, Mother and Uncle Drew said something to each other that I couldn't hear. The next thing I knew Uncle Drew was saying, "Welcome to Dalton, Tom," as he gave me an awkward, one-armed hug.

I knew that he had been holding something in his right hand when I first caught sight of him. I could smell the tobacco on his clothes and I understood that he was hiding a lighted cigar behind his back. I felt myself filling with pity and scorn for them all if they thought I must be shielded from this revelation of wickedness. I had tried to smoke a cigar myself once in Shanghai after finding a longish stub on the Bund. I hadn't liked it and I hadn't said anything in the front of the house. I took three or four swigs of tea in the kitchen to get rid of the taste, but I had remained unsmirched. And here were these innocents thinking to protect me.

3 ॐ

I REACHED VEGAS a little before noon and headed into a Standard
Oil filling station across from a liquor store. After I'd asked the
attendant to fill the tank and check everything, saying that the
Chevy might take a quart of oil, I used the men's room before I
crossed the street. In the liquor store I bought a fifth of scotch—
Teacher's, to be precise.

I found three quarters in my change, so I stopped at the row of
slot machines by the door. I lost the first quarter. On the second I got
back three. On the third, fourth, and fifth pulls I lost again. With one
quarter left I pulled the lever down hard just to make the wait longer
and watched the spinning fruits. I got back five quarters. That put
me fifty cents ahead.

I hadn't noticed that the man behind the counter had moved
down and was watching me until he asked, "You quitting already,
bud?"

"That's right. I'm ahead."

"Not by much," he said.

"No, but I'm still ahead, and that's something."

"I guess that's one way to live," he said.

"No," I said, "it's a way to eat."

"And drink?"

"If you're careful," I said. "But not now. Dear Teacher is for the
dry lands to the east."

"You from California?"

"I live there."

"I can usually tell," he said.

"But not too much," I said, heading for the door.

"Be seeing you," he said.

"Don't wait up," I said, smiling as I turned my head, and he smiled back. Back at the filling station the attendant had finished adding the quart of oil. I handed him my credit card, which he looked at closely. "We get more and more of these," he said. "You know, I never thought they'd catch on, they want so much information about you. Hey, you've had this for ten years!"

"Right," I said. "It was harder to get that card than it was to get married."

He snorted. "Guess you're right, especially in this town."

I could see he was wondering about my driving a well used Chevy if I qualified for a credit card, so I came out with a sure clincher. "Actually, I'm lucky. I have connections."

He nodded and said, "It figures."

While he wrote up the slip I put the Teacher's in the trunk. Then I unwrapped the corned beef sandwich I had made that morning and put it and an apple on the seat beside me after I got behind the wheel.

"You in that much of a hurry?" he asked as he handed me the slip to sign.

"I just like to eat while I drive," I said.

"Vegas is a good eating town," he said. "You eat cheap because they figure you'll more than pay at the tables or leave it in the machines."

"Another day."

"Which way you heading?"

"North," I said. "North and east—Wyoming for starters."

"That's a godforsaken land."

"Depends on how you look at it," I said.

"It's cold up there. You got anti-freeze?"

"Sure thing," I said, "right up to my neck."

He laughed. "Well, good luck."

"And to you," I said as I turned the key in the ignition.

Driving out of town, I thought of these ritual exchanges. They gave me a sense of achievement, an indication of how far I had come from that summer in Dalton, when it seemed to me that every time I opened my mouth I either amused or astonished a Lloyd or a Burr or a townsperson. When I couldn't think of a thing to say, it was even worse. But now I could handle this sort of thing almost automatically, and I could flatten out the "international" accent that Fran and I still use when we speak naturally. This may not be the art of conversation, but it's at least a hard-won way of getting along without calling attention to yourself—or, for that matter, risk actually saying something.

Some miles out on the road and with the Chevy settled to the gradual climb leading northeast, I reached over for my sandwich and took a bite. This was a holdover from our first crossing of the continent in the Model T, with a sandwich and a piece of fruit eaten on the road to save time and money. And then came the feeling of sated fullness after eating, rocking along, drowsy in the heat. I had to guard against that part now.

Not that we managed that ideal every day, or even every other day. More often than not, we had a flat about the time everyone was getting hungry. While Father patched the tube, Mother, Fran, and I would munch down our food in what shade we could find. Then Father would take a few minutes to eat before we drove on.

But the Platonic idea of a day's touring called for eating on the move. When we succeeded in this, Fran and I dozed in an aura of special virtue, even if we had to request stops later on for what I learned that summer in Dalton to call "the bodily functions." Until then I had spoken of them specifically without thinking, though in Chinese; for in these instances (to regress to the mission "style") the usages of the back of the house penetrated beyond their normal bounds. What pious jargon!

And now, after the long climb and with the untempting attractions of Mesquite behind me, I entered that brief passage between possible escapes as the highway cut across the northwestern corner of Arizona. Escapes to be rejected, but always there so long as you failed to test them.

Entering this foreign territory, accented by the state line marker, knowing that you must leave it in a matter of miles, you see off to the southwest a magic land. Sweeping slopes rise to high reddish mesas crowned with buttes that complete the design and require no pagodas from man. Beneath that pale blue sky, cloud flecked, with the winter sun already stretching the lavender shadows, you can believe for a few minutes that you could ride off into that land forever, or into the embrace of a society that will enclose and nourish you, both for you and for itself.

You may feel it cruel to bring it tumbling down as you skirt the Virgin River at Littlefield and gaze at the Virgin Mountains. But Littlefield, with its junkyard of wrecked, discarded cars, brings it down on its own. And bring it down you must or be forever lost. Actually, any map that Father would put his faith in would show that there isn't too much space to ride into over there—hardly enough to sustain a vision of paradise or eternity—because, given food and water, you would cross the Grand Wash and come up short at the Grand Canyon. But as long as you don't test it, it's there for you to cherish.

You have to be ready not only to bring it down but to shift into straight farce, because as you move through this magic corner, this private hypotenuse, you swing up, up and away, and there you are with the lost tribe of the Shivwitz. It's almost too much, and it's a good thing you haven't taken a slug of Teacher's yet, or you might pass out laughing or die from piling up on the road.

I hit the brakes full on as I came off a curve and caught sight of an Indian wagon crossing the right of way. An old man led his rough-haired pony by the headstall, and the woman, her full skirt dusty, followed. She must have closed the wire gate on the east side of the road, and now she shuffled ahead to open the gate on the west. My wheels locked and the Chevy stopped after a short diagonal skid. I waited for them to clear the way. The man looked back after he had climbed up on the seat and driven through the gate, waiting for his woman to catch up. I smiled and waved, an evangel of love and truth and brotherhood, once again the son of the mission. At first I thought he made no sign as they drove off, not turning to look at me, but then I saw he had his left hand up, the middle finger giving me his personal pagoda in the international code.

Oh, well! That was, indeed, that. I knew I could turn neither to the delectable mountains nor shack up with the Shivwitz. I was on my way to Dalton. And long before I got to Dalton I must leave my magic corner, the road climbing, then swinging into a valley, and there stood the pagoda of St. George, courtesy of the Angel Moroni. I knew that Zion thundered off to the east. All the public symbols were so blatant; only private mysteries satisfied. Help! I thought; I'm beginning to think like a literary critic with a system—one of the last deluded totalitarians of the West.

That first night in Dalton after our train trip I wasn't thinking like anyone but myself, unless it would be Fran. My amusement over the innocence of Mother and Uncle Drew, thinking they could fool me about his cigar, colored my memories of that first night in Grandfather Lloyd's house.

It started with meeting Grandma Tessy. Her bedroom projected over the front porch—not that I noticed that the first night—and she had prepared herself to receive us. Propped against a bank of pillows with lace-edged cases, her hair frizzed, and with a touch of rouge on each cheek, she didn't look very sick to me.

She opened her arms to Mother and Fran. Then it was my turn. I found the smell of perfume and powder attractive and disturbing, but even more unsettling was the expanse of firm bust her peignoir exposed and against which I found my face crushed. It wasn't that I didn't know what women's breasts looked like. I had seen both Chinese and foreign infants suckled in public and private ever since I could remember anything. I'd even had mother's milk laughingly squirted into my eyes, but this display was somehow a different kind of exposure.

I pulled back when I felt her hold loosen.

"So this is the tongue-tied Tom?"

"I guess so," I said.

"We'll have to get to know each other better, won't we?" she asked, running her tongue over her lips.

"Oh, yes indeed, Grandma Tessy," I said, though I wondered what getting to know her better could mean.

"Oh, yes indeed," she mimicked.

Her hands held my shoulders now, and she almost squinted at me. "Ah, let me see," she said, as she brought her right hand off my shoulder and up to her forehead, as if she had a headache. "Yes, there's more than just a touch of it, isn't there, Emma?" she said to Mother, her eyes leaving my face and looking behind me.

"Well . . . " Mother began.

"Yes, a distinct touch of it around the eyes—ah, the eyes!" she said, and now her hand came down from her forehead and covered her own eyes.

It was like watching a stage play.

She took a deep, trembling breath. "I must control myself," she said, "for the sake of us all."

"Yes, Tessy," Mother said without emphasis.

"I know they've saved something for you in the kitchen, and I mustn't be selfish and keep you because everyone is waiting to see you. And I must rest, of course, I must rest," she said with more of the funny differences in her speech I had heard on the telephone. I saw the phone itself now on her nightstand. She leaned back into the pillows, breathing heavily, her eyes closed.

"Yes, Tessy, you must take care of yourself," Mother said in a level tone. "It's true, the children must be starved."

I hadn't pictured eating in the kitchen in America. It was a huge room, jammed now with Lloyds and Burrs. I saw two older boys that I knew must be my cousins Brooks and Rob, Uncle Drew's sons. They came over to me and Brooks said, "Well, Tom, how would you like to have some chow?"

"That would be very nice," I said.

"Very nice," Brooks said, his lips curved, and I knew that he, like Grandma Tessy, was imitating my accent.

"How about some fried chicken?" Brooks asked. "Some fried chicken and slaw, that's always a good pair. Of course, it's just cold fried chicken."

"Cold fried chicken?"

"Cold fried chicken," he repeated, again aping me.

"What piece do you like best?" Rob asked.

"I don't know," I said. "I've never had anything but a drumstick."

They both grinned and Brooks snorted. "Well, now's your chance to experiment—go wild," he said. "Say, I'll just pick what *I* think you'd like. Back in a sec."

Rob, though he was a year and a half younger than Brooks, stood a bit taller and was heavier than his brother. "I know how you feel," he said. "Funny how all boys are supposed to go for the same thing."

"Go for?"

"Like," he said. "Don't mind Brooks. He always teases. Right now maybe more than usual because . . . " He hesitated, then went on, "I guess you know about the bank?"

"Yes."

"You see, Brooks feels it a lot because he's always been the leader of the boys in town."

"Sure," I said, just to be polite. I didn't know what he meant.

Brooks came back and handed me a plate full of food and a fork and a napkin. "I don't know how you eat chicken with chopsticks over in Shanghai," he said, "but here in our great republic we use our fingers on informal family occasions."

I picked up and bit into the piece of solid white meat and chewed. If this was the new Jerusalem it wasn't too bad. I tried a forkful of slaw, which was new to me, and that tasted good too. But with my second mouthful of the moist white meat I thought of Grandma Tessy and felt uneasy, remembering my mouth pressed against her, my nose jammed between her powdered breasts. It wasn't, I suspected, anything I could report to the front of the house.

Everyone stood, holding a plate, and across the room Uncle Drew was telling a story I could tell was meant to be funny, even though I couldn't catch the words. Fran stood with Martha, Aunt Louise's daughter, who was a couple of years older than Fran. Through all the talk I heard Mother saying to Aunt Louise, "Tessy hasn't changed at all, has she?" And Aunt Louise said, "You didn't expect her to, did you?" Mother made some kind of face and said something I couldn't catch as Uncle Drew's story ended in an explosion of laughter.

A little later Brooks brought me a dish of ice cream. He and Rob flanked me and we began that awkward exchange between boys a little too far apart in age, not to mention a lot of other things, to be easy with each other.

"What's it like living in China?" Brooks asked.

"I guess I don't know," I said. "I've never lived anywhere else to remember that's . . . " I stopped, because I was going to say that it was home, when here, after all the waiting, I really was "home."

"I suppose that's right," Rob said. "We'll have to show you around."

"That would be nice," I said.

"All the boys sort of hang out together during the summer," Brooks said.

"I see," I said, though I didn't and I wondered what he meant by "hang out."

"Yeah," Rob said. "You come with us and you'll get to know everybody in the club."

"I think I'd like that."

Then it was time for bed. Fran and I said goodnight to a lot of people I couldn't keep straight. Mother took us upstairs to one of the side bedrooms, where she and Fran would have the double bed and I had a cot in an alcove that must have been planned for a dressing room.

I put my things away in a small chest of drawers before I undressed. For a few moments I fondled my American money in the pair of rolled up stockings.

After we'd been to the bathroom, Mother left. When we went to bed I could hear voices coming up from the kitchen.

Then Fran called softly from the other room, "Tom, can you hear me?"

"Yes."

"Do you know what *moonshine* means?" she asked.

"Gee!" I said, "I guess I do if you don't mean moon*light*." Fran hadn't sounded very confident. Having her actually ask me about something was a change. I got out of bed and went into the room.

"No, it couldn't be that," she said. "What are you doing?"

"I thought it would be easier to talk in here," I said and slid under the sheet on the other side of the bed.

"That's not a bad idea," Fran said. When we had been younger we had had our twin beds side by side in the old upstairs nursery in Shanghai. Sometimes we deliberately scared ourselves when we heard noises outside or imagined them inside if the servants had gone to their quarters, and then we would hold hands before we went to sleep. That was before we had our own rooms. I knew Fran wouldn't like if it I tried to hold her hand now.

"Well, what *does* moonshine mean?" she demanded.

"I don't know if I should tell you," I said, thinking that this was a kind of male knowledge and remembering how she had laughed about the pagodas.

"Why not?"

"You won't let Mother know I know?"

"Of course not."

"Well, then," I said, relenting, "it means alcohol, homemade alcohol to drink, you know. It's against the law. Sometimes it's also called *hooch*."

"What a funny word! How do you know all this?

"I heard some men talking about it on the *Empress of Asia*."

"I still don't understand," she said.

"Understand what?"

"Uncle Drew's story that everyone laughed at. It had something to do with moonshine."

"Can't you remember any of it?"

"Not really, but I suppose it meant someone was drunk."

"Probably," I said. "Did you hear Mother and Aunt Louise talking about Grandma Tessy?"

"No. What did they say?"

"Not much," I said, "just that she hadn't changed. Does that mean she's been in bed all the time we were in China?"

"I don't think so, but I'm not sure."

I felt a kind of sad feeling to hear Fran admit twice now that she didn't know about something. She was always the one who knew about things, and I depended on her.

After a while I ventured, "Now that we're here, what do you think about everything?"

She said nothing for a long time. Her voice had recovered its old authority when she did speak. "I'm not so sure that this is our real home."

She had said it. "I know how you feel," I said. I still knew I couldn't touch her hand and I didn't want to now because I thought once more of the white chicken meat and Grandma Tessy. At last the noise from downstairs grew less. I could tell Fran had fallen asleep. I slid out of the bed, pulled the covers on that side straight and went back to my cot.

That was everything I remembered about our first night in Dalton. I couldn't even be sure what day of the week it had been, but certainly not a Sunday.

I had been driving automatically. Coming back to a sense of place and time I felt cold and hungry and I knew, not that I hadn't always known, that I had set my sights a notch too high. I had my secret plan. What is the point of going anywhere without a secret plan?

Maybe if I ate, if I sneaked a drink in this God-driven country, I could improvise a variation. I brooded over this as I drove north through Utah. Coming into Cedar City, the Chevy's headlights on, I knew I must discard my first plan, which had been to cut across the valley either here or above at Beaver and work east by back roads. Instead, I must eat here and head north to be ready for the next day's drive. The whole grandly impossible idea had been to do it all, to get all the way to Wyoming, without a pause—too extravagant from the start.

I stopped across from a hotel that advertised a dining room, and got the bottle of Teacher's out of the trunk. In the passenger's seat I put the bottle to my lips after I'd opened it and took a good long pull, holding it in my mouth for a few seconds before I let it burn down my throat. I took another pull right after the first, making it almost a rite in this land of channeled water and virtue.

Before I felt the liquor, I locked the Chevy and crossed over to the hotel. In the dining room the red-checked tablecloths reminded me that the big kitchen table in Dalton had been covered with yellow-checked oilcloth. As I ordered the standard fare from the standard menu I felt the warmth rising through me and thought of my plan.

It wasn't anything world-shaking. And it didn't depend on doing the whole trip in one day. All I needed to do to satisfy a boyhood yearning was drive from Green River in Utah to Green River in Wyoming. When Father had looked at my map I had expected him to comment on my apparent indecision shown by the variant blue tracings, but I understood now that he hadn't really examined any of this as soon as he learned it lacked the Auto Club's authority.

Coming out into the cold air, I knew the sensible thing was to put up at the hotel and wait for morning. But the whisky had lifted me. I took another drag before I locked the bottle in the trunk and started the engine. After turning up the heater, I flicked on the radio. After some scratchiness I brought in a Salt Lake station. Instead of the news and the weather that I wanted, I heard a commercial followed by a selection of choral music.

Part of the ritual was never to ask for outside help. Once I had returned from my memories of Dalton I had seen some dull white on the mountains to my right. That probably meant snow, canceling the first of the blue lines on my map. For the first part of this next leg I would drive on north, even if this meant some backtracking.

Against this prudence and the choral music I felt the slow harsh music of the placenames as I drove on through the night, my headlights picking up the signs. I noted the turnoff to Enoch and later I passed through Summit and Parowan, Paragonah and—after a long break—Beaver. They created their own rhythm, one that cried out for a latter-day Blake or Whitman to give them voice. Manderfield and Cove Fort joined the line.

Stopping in Cove Fort, I pulled up and got the Teacher's again, turning on the dome light and checking my map. I saw that instead of backtracking I could try a riskier variant that would let me drive through Green River, Utah, the next day and go on into Colorado before turning north to come back into Utah and reach Vernal, where a thin line led through the mountains to the other Green River—the one in Wyoming.

I was thrown back into my greenest youth, when I'd had to memorize and declaim a certain number of poems, "Green River" among them. I couldn't remember just when I had realized with an inner flush of embarrassment that the Green River I had found in my American geography book could hardly be the stream beside which William Cullen Bryant had stolen an hour from study and care. Looking more closely, I saw not only the Western Green River but the two towns, all in that mysterious, secret West. The discovery haunted me, and later in college, when I found there was actually a soft drink called Green River, I used to order it, though it never did what Teacher's could.

One thing Amy had said before I left was, "Try to relax, Tom. You know, get back sometimes just to what you want to do. Forget about the rest of us for a while."

I had nodded, and thought of this private wish. So here I was, stowing the bottle again and once more driving, coasting along on the fumes of whisky and memories of Dalton. The music stopped and a weather report mentioned recent snow that had cleared. I floated through Richfield, through Sigurd and Aurora, on to Salina.

The headlights began to pick up white patches beside the road.

Tired now after the long day of past and present, I pulled into the first decent-looking motel that I came to in Salina. Not that there could be any motels in this land that wouldn't be called decent.

The middle-aged man who came out in response to my touch on the night bell looked puzzled while he rubbed the sleep out of his eyes.

"You're real late," he said.

"Late?" I echoed, still partly in the past. "I don't have a reservation. You must be expecting somebody else."

"No, I'm not expecting anyone," he said. "I just mean it's late to be out driving."

"Sorry," I said. "I wasn't trying to be smart."

"No offense," he said.

And there I was again, entering into my final American ritual exchange of the day. I pulled myself together. "You get much traffic this time of year?" I asked as I filled out the registration card.

"Not much," he said. "Of course there's always some through drivers and truckers."

"I suppose," I said.

"You on your way back to California?" he asked, looking at the card.

"No, from," I said.

"You may be asking for it tomorrow," he said. "Three doors down on the left. You know, I thought of turning off the sign an hour ago and then I layed out on the couch and got the Salt Lake station. I must have dozed."

"Makes sense," I said.

"I can turn on the heater for you if you like."

"Don't bother," I said. "I can manage if I need it."

"Sure," he said. "It's a hard time of year for going east."

"It's on family business," I said.

"Oh well, then, of course," he said.

"That's right. No getting away from it."

"I can see that," he said. "Have a good sleep."

"You, too," I said, feeling that I had come to the end of a perfectly executed fugue. "American Fugue," Number 3.

I unlocked the door and took my briefcase and suitcase in with me. Then I went back to the Chevy and picked up the Teacher's. I put it on the nightstand beside the Book of Mormon. Even if I hadn't made it all the way in one day, from Elizabeth Street in Pasadena to a motel in Salina with a bottle of Teacher's and the Book of Mormon stood for a considerable leap.

I saw that the heater was the kind that would need hours to warm the room, so I ignored it. I took the extra blanket from the foot of the bed once I was in my pajamas. I pulled down the sheet and blanket already on the bed and spread the other blanket out. I rolled up in it. Before I pulled the covers over me I took a long last drag of Teacher's and turned out the light. I shivered until the blanket held my body heat. I kept wondering what day of the week it had been that we'd arrived in Dalton, but after a while I held it all suspended as the whisky and sleep took me together.

4 ❧

I AWOKE TO darkness, alert to the importance of fixing the day of the week we got to Dalton. It wasn't Sunday, because the first Sunday in Dalton had turned into one of the longest, most confusing days of my life. So it must have been early in the week, because I'd picked up a lot of information between arriving and that Sunday morning. I knew that Aunt Netty, who was Mother's half-sister, had the big room across the upstairs hall from us. In what had been that dressing room stood a crib for Kenny, Aunt Floss's motherless baby, Aunt Floss having been Aunt Netty's full sister, and therefore Mother's half-sister.

I knew that Uncle Drew, who was Mother's younger brother, and his wife, Aunt Harriet, lived with their sons, Brooks and Rob, in Dalton's only "modern bungalow"—all the rooms on one floor— two blocks east of the Lloyd house. And I knew that Aunt Louise, Mother's oldest sister, and Uncle Fred and their daughter Martha occupied a big, sparsely furnished apartment above the International Harvester showrooms on Main Street.

I knew, too, that at the Lloyd house a Mrs. Hauser, who wasn't exactly a servant, came in almost every day and "helped." Mrs. Hauser talked freely with Mother and Aunt Louise, sometimes using their first names, but her daughter, Heidi, a year older than Fran, wasn't treated quite the same as the other children. Though I hadn't seen it, I knew Mrs. Hauser lived in an old caboose that had been lifted off the railroad tracks and put up on blocks in a vacant lot on the other side of the tracks.

I wasn't sure, staring into the dark, if I already knew by then that

Heidi was Mrs. Hauser's youngest child, that she had two older half-brothers—almost grown men. I was sure I hadn't yet learned that each of Mrs. Hauser's children had a different father, but I did know that Mrs. Hauser and Heidi went to the Catholic church.

"Is the Presbyterian church a long walk from here?" I had asked Mother that first Sunday after breakfast.

"It would be a very long walk to get to a Presbyterian church," Mother said. "Dalton has just three churches—a Catholic one, a Baptist one that we'll be going to, and a Methodist one."

I started to sweat as we walked the four blocks to the Baptist Church. Inside, the church was dark and cool. It was only a third or less filled by the time the service began. The first time a man called out "Amen!" from a pew behind us I started and looked around. Mother touched my shoulder and shook her head. When someone else came out with a ringing "That's the Lord's own truth!" I wondered if Mother hadn't made a mistake. I hadn't seen any of my cousins, though out of the corner of my eye I caught a glimpse of a man I felt pretty certain was a Burr. If the Burrs came to a place like this, I couldn't think they amounted to much even if they did come from Virginia.

I leaned forward slowly, hoping to catch Fran's eye. Mother sat between us, and when I got my head out far enough I saw Fran sitting with her most frozenly condescending expression holding her face in control. I knew she knew I was trying to catch her eye and that she wouldn't let me. So I pulled back slowly and tried to settle comfortably against the wooden back of the pew.

After all, I was an experienced minister's and missionary's child. I had logged hours and hours of services and sermons, including high-class sermons in literary Chinese that I couldn't have understood more than a word or two of even if I'd listened.

But when we stood to sing "From Greenland's Icy Mountains to India's Torrid Plain"—and I listened approvingly to my own clear soprano carrying high and sweet as I pointedly refused to use a hymnal—I saw that the Dalton Baptist Church offered a real challenge. Even plainer than most of the church interiors I was used to, it limited the old standby counting games, the adding up of panes of glass according to color or size or shape with calculations of addition, division, and multiplication to do in my head. There was a chance, though, that I might be able to use each head of the congregation if I made knight's moves, if possible without repeats. It would take some doing, and I might have to relax the rules here and there, which would probably be all right in a Baptist church.

After we sat down, the collection plates passed along the rows with a lot of stretching and reaching. Fran and I had to tithe out of our allowances, and while I fished a nickel out of one of my pockets I thought of my hidden American money. Maybe I could put my plug nickel in some Sunday. Surely the Lord could redeem whatever of worth was in it. Or would He be angry? It might be a greater sin to give it to God than to Caesar. I thought of Ananias and decided to play it safe.

Even when the sermon started I found the pattern a little strange and almost yielded to the temptation of listening to see if I could tell why it sounded odd. I was considering my first knight's move when the minister's voice shot up on something about "our dear sister" and later "circumstances of sorrow," an unusual phrase, I thought. Mother must have thought so too, because she shifted in the pew.

While I brooded over whether it would be all right to change the rule about jumping the center aisle, the minister's voice rose again with "the hymn we have especially sung," and I knew he must be desperate for something to say if he had to talk about a hymn instead of expounding Holy Writ. Again he called out "our dear sister," distracting me from my game.

Before I started it I had to turn around to see the heads behind me, always a tricky problem. Should I jerk my head around fast, as if something important had happened to make it all right to look back, or should I make a slow-moving arc that might not be noticed? I'd begun the second, safer move when someone behind me called out, "Oh, truly, truly, good Lord!" and I whipped my head around because this was my idea of a real disturbance. Mother's hand touched my leg, but as I brought my head back slowly, hoping I wouldn't blush, I had seen the whole pattern behind me on the other side of the aisle.

Then a lot of persons laughed right out loud, and I saw Mother smiling and wiping her eyes. From my ear's memory I tried to get back the words causing this scandal, but all I could remember was "the day she rode bareback before the advancing rainstorm." It sounded a bit like Revelations, but not violent enough. I couldn't help wondering how Mother could think this place was a proper church—it could hardly be even a pagoda in disguise.

I let my head turn slowly the other way to complete my survey. The minister was saying, "soon call upon our dearly beloved sister in the faith to say a few words," and thought how silly he sounded.

Mother said, "Oh dear!" under her breath and I saw her hands tighten in her lap. Then I knew for sure something had gone wrong, because Mother stood up. I couldn't believe that even Baptists would be satisfied with such a short sermon, but I felt happy and jumped up myself, ready to leave. She pressed my shoulder and whispered, "No, Tom, just stay here with Fran." And Fran glared at me as Mother stepped into the aisle.

The minister announced, "Our dear Sister Jerome," as if Mother was a Catholic, and an awful thing happened. Everyone began clapping in this crazy House of the Lord. Why, it wasn't even a pagoda! I felt sick. But I knew my part. I clasped my hands tight in my lap, stiffened my back, and lifted my head to a slight upward angle, knowing I wore my best, my very best mouth expression—a sort of hint of a beginning of a smile, but still reverent.

In public, Mother's voice lost the quiet tone she used at home, deferring to Father. She spoke right up. I listened now as she said something about the joys of returning home, which was strange because she didn't sound joyful. Then she said something about "The Work" in Shanghai. Whenever Mother and Father spoke about "The Work" it led into the saving of souls, and that worried me. Neither the cook nor the amah had been saved, which bothered Father especially, because they were the best servants in the whole compound and they weren't Presbyterians or even converts to one of the lesser sects. I missed a lot of what Mother said, and the next words that came through turned into something about "a family given to service and sacrifice." A regular hum started up and I supposed they were thinking of Old Testament blood sacrifices, which seemed stupid, but a few "Amens!" came out of the hum and I saw Mother flush as she added, "Judge not that ye be not judged," and that was out of the Bible for sure, and then she added something about "knowledge of good and evil spared the very young," which didn't quite make sense because it was connected with the Garden of Eden.

The people in front of us turned their heads and looked at Fran and me, and I was conceited enough to think that more of them noticed me than her. I could tell from her upper lip that she was furious. But they faced forward again and now I knew that Fran and I were together, not only because of the rudeness of being stared at but because we both saw what was happening to Mother. She may not have wanted to speak, but once started, her voice grew more and more confident and she had obviously begun to enjoy the chance to say something. We both knew she would be hard to stop, but I didn't care in this loose sort of place, though I suspected that Fran felt embarrassed.

Yes, Fran and I were together again, frozen in our mission-child-in-public postures, feeling the burdens that life put upon us in demanding this pluperfect—I'd gotten that far in grammar and liked the word—behavior.

Mother was saying something about charity, but she didn't sound a bit charitable, and that was pretty funny. The people we could see in front of us stirred a bit and there was some headshaking, and the minister began edging up towards Mother. She noticed this and smiled in his direction as she said, "You can't stop me until I've made it clear in spite of some of the things I've said that I want this home-coming to be a true homecoming for us all in every way, not only for me, but also for my children to come to know you, their own people, and I know in my heart that all of you in your Christian love will help us in this." Then she said, "Thank you one and all," and, leaving the lectern, stepped down and came up the aisle briskly.

A real round of blasphemous applause defiled this presumably holy place. Confused by it, I decided at the last moment that I should get out in the aisle and let Mother in to the pew. We almost crashed into each other, but she said, "Thank you, Tom, that's very nice of you," which made me feel better.

I knew that she had been mixed up because she must have meant the Lloyds and Burrs when she said "their own people." I thought I would point this out to Fran later, if she hadn't caught it herself, but right now she was working herself up into her best martyrdom pose. Her head kept getting a nobler and nobler tilt, and all I could hope was that she wouldn't get so completely noble that she'd refuse to speak to me when the service ended.

Now that the minister was at it again, I started my knight's move game with a straw-hatted old lady down in front on my left. From there I had two choices—a bald man, or a boy with hair that had been wetted down but was now starting to spring up in short red tufts like someone I couldn't quite remember the name of in a Dickens story.

I had let the whole thing go too late. I'd made only five moves when everyone stood up and we sang "A mighty fortress is our God," and then came the Doxology correctly enough, and the organist shifted into something lively to move everyone out. Here we were ready, but Mother held us back until all those in front had passed us. I watched for the red-haired boy. He looked about my age and I wondered if I would get to know him and if I could tell him we had a bond because I had picked him for my first knight's move.

The sun really bit into us as we walked back to the house.

"Is it always this hot in the summer here?" I asked.

"Oh, pretty much," Mother said.

"Why don't people go away to the mountains or the beach?"

"Tom, you don't know what you're talking about," Fran said, dropping all her nobility.

"I'm not talking about anything," I said. "I was just asking a question."

"Yes," she snapped, "but your question showed you don't know anything about it."

"That's why I asked a question," I said. "You couldn't say I was talking about anything when I was asking a question, could you?"

"Now, you two," Mother said, "stop carrying on like that. What Tom said about the heat makes some sense because it can get on your nerves. But no, Tom, people don't go away for the summer here, especially now. It's a busy time for farmers, and about all anyone does is get to Chicago for a few days or just take a day trip to Lakeview. I'm glad you and Fran are going to learn how your own people live, the sort of people you may be with when you come to America to college on your own."

"I don't need to know all this," Fran said, "because I've already learned it and I'd just as soon go back."

I was glad Fran was talking, because I had to deal with what Mother had just said. She had really meant that all those Amen shouters and handclappers, profaners of the Lord's House, were "our own people"! That we could be walking along in the moist heat as if nothing had happened was just as scandalous, but perhaps I was the only person there who knew something frightful had happened. That made me feel better and I smiled to myself. I could see how annoyed Fran was getting when she saw me walking along, sweating, with my secret smile on my face.

She couldn't say anything about it, so I made my smile even better and more secret. Fran dropped back so Mother was exactly between us and Fran couldn't see me.

Then I knew I could easily get lost in Dalton without Fran and I began to worry. I tried to think of something stupid to say. We were getting close to the cement walk up to the house, flanked by two tall trees. I said, "I don't suppose since everyone's so poor now that there'll be much to eat for Sunday dinner, will there?"

That turned out perfectly, because Fran giggled. "That just shows how much you know about nothing, Tom."

Mother was trying not to laugh herself, making a sort of choking sound, and for an instant I thought it would be awful if they both began to shriek hysterically on the sidewalk at high noon on a Sunday outside the Lloyd house.

Luckily, nothing quite like that happened. Mother got hold of her voice and as we went up between the two trees she said, "I know it's hard to understand, Tom, but you mustn't fret over starving, and certainly not today."

"Of course we won't starve, Tom," Fran chimed in. "You say the silliest things sometimes."

"I guess so," I said, feeling much better.

Mother and Fran walked straight back to the kitchen where Aunt Louise and Mrs. Hauser stood talking and Mother said, "I know you'll laugh when I tell you that Tom . . . "

I went upstairs without waiting to hear the rest, feeling pretty good about keeping in touch with Fran and still beating her to the bathroom.

And all that, I knew now, staring into the darkness of the motel room, was why I had wondered about the day of the week that we got to Dalton. I thought of taking another pull of Teacher's, but then I began to drowse with a sense of content. I rolled over in my blanket and drifted off through broken memories of Dalton.

5 ❧

I AWOKE THE second time to whiteness seeping in around the shades, and with a spurt of boyish delight thought it might have snowed while I slept. After I wriggled out of my cocoon and pulled back the curtains I saw that it wasn't snow, after all, but a heavy frost.

I shaved quickly. Pulling on my clothes, looking at the bottle of Teacher's beside the Book of Mormon—"Still Life in Central Utah" —I felt the weight of Dalton partly lifted from me.

After dressing and packing, I walked across the street to a cafe. A couple of truck drivers held mugs of coffee at the counter and I took a seat a little way down from them. One of them glanced at me and turned to say something to the other. The second man pulled his head back to look down the counter, just in time to catch my eye on him, my best mission smile on my face. I waved to him and nodded. He ducked back, but not without a jerky move of his hand in response.

I could see myself in the mottled mirror behind the service area and still watch the drivers. What they had probably agreed on was that I was no truck driver. I would give them no argument there. But I had my own style by now, one that I must have begun to shape long ago in the Dalton days. I was still lanky, standing six-two when I troubled to straighten up, and I kept my dark brown hair an inch or so longer than the standard fashion. On my short upper lip I sported a mustache, neither clipped nor ragged. It went with the tweed jacket, the casual shirt—but never a buttoned-down collar—the oxford-gray slacks, and oxblood slip-on shoes for this morning hour. Like my accent, none of it was easy to place. All anyone usually risked was that I wasn't a native of wherever I happened to be.

I'd learned to anticipate a going-over and to get into it before anyone got to me. Just as I'd forced the second driver to respond, I knew I could now shift down the counter and start up a red-white-and-blue American conversation. "You men drive a regular route through here?" was the gambit for that and you went on, depending on how you felt, into schedules, diesel fuel, gears on grades, union rules and cops' attitude in one direction, or eating stops, distance between, coffee, food, and available "female company" in the other.

I didn't feel like getting into either sequence this morning, so I kept my eyebrows up a little and assumed a tolerant expression. I'd learned to use my tongue as weapon or shield. I'd picked up and turned around the satiric touch, the note of parody I got so often in Dalton that summer. If anyone cared to take on this slightly foreign-looking, but somehow very native American, he'd find that he him-self was somehow the major source of amusement.

It could be entertaining, especially in the larger context of every-day life as parody, though few persons recognize themselves as parodies, and that can make for problems.

Even if I didn't want to play the game with the drivers I could still reach them through the mirror as the waitress, pushing her hair back under her starched bandeau, listened to my order: a glass of orange juice, a sweet roll, and black coffee.

"You get much custom this time of year?" I asked.

"Not much," she said. In the mirror I saw the men exchange glances.

"I shouldn't have expected you to." Her ring finger showed the mark of a wedding band. I wondered if she put it back on after hours. "Still, you must have some stop-off regulars with a highway like this," I went on.

"Sure thing," she said. She glanced down the counter at the drivers. I thought of my Dalton cousins as the mirror showed the farther trucker trying to lift his eyebrows as he grinned at his partner. It wasn't a complete success. The waitress went down the counter to freshen their coffee mugs.

"You can always tell about the coffee and the food in a place like this if you see a couple of able-bodied drivers ordering," I went on relentlessly as she drifted back.

"That's what they say." Her hand went up to check the bandeau.

"And a good-looking girl," I continued, thinking, what the hell, you've got to make the whole trip once you've started.

"Oh, I wouldn't know about that," she said with a truly attractive smile, and then her eyes darted down the counter. The eyebrow lifter had lost his quizzical look. Both men looked puzzled. Could this character down the line know his way around, after all?

"Well, I'm sure there are others who do know," I said confidently. Nothing could stem our progress now.

She smiled again. "You like a little hot coffee, honey?"

Honey? This was almost too fast. "Just a few drops," I said, unwilling to add "baby" or "doll."

"You staying in town to sell something?" she came along.

"Afraid not this time," I said. "I've got to hit the road—family business, you know—but there's always the return trip."

"Sure thing," she said. I paid my check and left a quarter on the counter.

The drivers studied their coffee. I gave them each a pat on the back as I walked behind them. "Have a good day on the road, pals," I said.

Flustered, they swung around and one of them managed to get out "Sure thing, bud."

I waved without turning back.

A good start for the day, but I needed gas and felt the old irritation as I drove into the first filling station I saw that I had a credit card for. By the time I'd signed the slip and started out on the road, the melting frost gave the countryside a mottled look. After some stretches over rounded slopes, the road gained intimacy, leading through narrow canyons and past craggy outcrops. Then the sky opened out, the land lifted, the turns grew wider and gentler. Another hour or so would bring me to my dream river.

Considering what I'd had for breakfast, I couldn't understand why I felt close to queasy until I realized that my memory had already taken me back to that first Sunday in Dalton.

When I came downstairs after church I walked into the kitchen where Mother and Aunt Louise were still talking. The yellow oil cloth on the table was almost invisible, cluttered by so many pots and pans and different dishes. I saw that the door of the short pantryway leading to the dining room stood open. I had scarcely been into the dining room until now. The sitting room at the front of the house I had inspected, drawn by a collection of oddments arranged on a bamboo étagère—a miniature bale of cotton from the Chicago Fair, a Chinese silver rickshaw pulled by a silver rickshaw boy that Mother must have sent from Shanghai, some arrowheads, a Japanese lacquer box, a piece of cloisonné work, souvenir teaspoons, some embroidered samplers.

The dining room hadn't interested me until now. A starched Irish linen tablecloth in the chrysanthemum pattern covered the table that had been lengthened by many leaves. Mother must have sent this from China, because we had one like it in Shanghai. We bought all our Irish linen "at a family discount" through a very distant Scotch-Irish cousin of Father's who lived with her husband and two sons in the International Settlement.

As I looked at the table I knew that almost all the Lloyd connections must be coming. Place after place was set with off-white, heavy china stamped in a blue medallion pattern, an exact duplicate of the china we used for family breakfasts in Shanghai and called "the ordinary blue set." Seeing it there ready for the dignity of Sunday dinner, I thought of how the cook would have laughed at this upgrading, because our tableboy would have brought out the set of gold-rimmed Haviland for a serious occasion.

Aunt Louise saw me as I walked back into the hot kitchen. "Really, Tom," she said, "you ought to have enough faith, especially on a Sunday, to believe that you'd get your daily bread."

"Certainly, Aunt Louise," I said. I knew better than to go on and say anything about not living by bread alone and asking why we seemed to have been the only members of the family to go to church, though I could understand that a Lloyd would probably feel a plain old Baptist church pretty low.

"After you've gone upstairs and freshened yourself," she said, "everyone will be coming and we'll see if we can't fill you up. You certainly look as if you needed it."

"Yes, thank you," I said. I couldn't say I'd already been upstairs, so I trudged back, stood in our room for a while and then started down again, wondering where Fran could be.

Standing at the top of the stairs once more, planning to step spang in the middle of the center diamond of the carpeting, I heard voices. Looking down, I saw Uncle Drew with Brooks and Rob and Aunt Harriet coming in through the front door, and Uncle Fred had turned up, wiping his mouth. When he caught sight of me up on the landing, he said something to Uncle Drew, who nodded.

I heard a thumping off to one side, and Grandma Tessy's voice calling "Come someone, please!" I went to her door and knocked and when she said "Come in," I opened it and there sat Grandma Tessy in bed, with a whole tray of bottles and powder boxes in front of her, looking at herself in a silver-backed hand mirror.

"Oh, it's you, Tom," she said. "You're a very mannerly boy, and that's nice. The way young people behave nowadays, and not just the young people, I might say, is a far cry from the Old Virginia ways I was brought up with. If you would bring me the green hand towel from the stand in my dressing room I would thank you very much for it."

I brought her the towel. "That's most kind of you, Tom," she said. "And is everyone coming for Sunday dinner?"

"It looks like it."

"Ah, almost like the old times," she said. "How I wish I were strong enough to be with you all."

"Everyone would like that, I'm sure."

"Oh, perhaps not everyone," she said, batting her eyes at me. "But I'd like to think *you* would, Tom."

"I'm sure I would."

"Stand right close to me here," she said. "I want to look well at you once more."

I took a step forward, hoping I wasn't going to have my nose plunged into her powdered cleavage again. Luckily, she kept staring into my eyes.

"I want us to be good friends, Tom. You know, I can see him, see your dear grandfather in your eyes."

I didn't know what to say. Then she leaned over the far side of the bed, her head off the pillows. Before I could move, she righted herself and I saw she held a fat roll of money. She fumbled with it half hidden under the sheet. Then she lurched over again and I knew she was tucking the roll under her mattress.

She straightened up and held out a dollar bill. "See, Tom, this is for you, just for you."

"For me?" I didn't know what to do.

"Just for you. It's a secret between us. You mustn't say anything about it to anyone else. It will be just *our* secret."

"Oh," I said, automatically taking the bill.

"Now you just tuck that into your pocket and pleasure yourself with it," she said.

"Oh, thank you, Grandma," I said, jamming the bill into a pants pocket.

She said, "I must wait till I'm stronger to go downstairs, but I hope they remember to send up a little tray for me."

I hadn't closed the door. Mrs. Hauser came in carrying quite a big tray.

"I shouldn't keep them waiting," I said, and Grandma Tessy said, "That's right," as she reached for her napkin.

Back in our room, I put the dollar with the money Mr. Carter had given me. I felt uneasy about not telling anyone as I went downstairs again.

Brooks and Rob came up to me and Brooks said, "Why don't we fix it so you can sit between us?"

"That would be very nice indeed," I said.

"Oh, very nice indeed, I'm sure," Brooks echoed me not too accurately. He still hadn't quite caught what Fran and I to this day call our "international accent," which isn't the way either Mother or Father spoke and isn't quite British either.

Abstracted, I thought now for a minute or two about that, keeping the car going smoothly through the highway's curves. Must I always define my life through negatives? I doubt if anything like that troubled me during that Sunday dinner—or perhaps it did.

We were a real crowd, with Uncle Drew at the head of the table, a turkey in front of him, and Aunt Louise at the foot, with a big ham in front of her, making it clear that the Lloyds ran this particular show.

I saw Mother signal Uncle Drew with her eyes and he gave it right back to her as he cleared his throat and said, "I know that for today we must all be especially happy to have Emma and Fran and Tom back with us. I feel it's only fitting that we ask Emma to return thanks."

"Return thanks" surprised me—not that I didn't understand the phrase, but I'd always thought, and I knew Fran agreed, that it wasn't a very polished way of speaking.

But Mother just said, "Certainly, Drew, if that's what you wish." She began to pray, but her voice came close to breaking soon and she stopped after saying "Amen" quietly. She dabbed at her eyes with a corner of her napkin, something Fran and I had been taught not to do. "I'm so sorry," Mother said.

Uncle Fred coughed. Uncle Drew stood up and looked straight at me. "What do you say, Tom, to our trying to fatten you up a little on some of this food?"

Almost everyone smiled. I felt uncomfortable, afraid he was really going to serve me first, so I said, "Thank you, Uncle Drew, but I can wait at least until the ladies are served."

They all acted as if that was a terribly witty remark and laughed a lot, though I noticed that Uncle Fred looked a bit sour. Then everyone began talking at once and I was relieved not to be the focus of attention any longer as Uncle Drew stood to carve the turkey. Aunt Louise, without rising, set about slicing the ham, while Mrs. Hauser shuttled back and forth in some clever way, getting turkey and ham onto a plate if that was what a person wanted, or just ham or just turkey. Almost everyone had been served when Aunt Louise looked around the table and said, "But where is Heidi, Mrs. Hauser, and where are your places and why isn't she here?"

"She's in the kitchen," Mrs. Hauser said. "I didn't think that with so many there would be room, and even so . . . "

"But of course there's room," Aunt Louise said. A great stir took over as chairs were pushed closer together and places shifted. Heidi came in from the kitchen and we had to have two more plates and my food was getting cold, though why I cared in that heat I couldn't say.

At last we could dig in and for a few minutes no one said anything except how good everything was and paid compliments to Aunt Louise, who said it was Mrs. Hauser who did the real work, and Mrs. Hauser would keep apologizing for something and Heidi, her blond hair curling over her ears, looked shy but kept up a good pace eating, glancing from time to time at Fran down the table from her and me almost directly across.

Uncle Drew asked me how I was getting along and I said, "Very nicely, sir, thank you." Almost everyone except Uncle Fred seemed to think that was pretty funny too. I couldn't help thinking they were easy to entertain.

In the middle of this we heard a thumping above one corner of the ceiling. Mrs. Hauser jumped up, saying, "It would be easier just to take up another plate," but Aunt Louise, looking at Aunt Netty, said, "That might offend her, she's so delicate, you know." Not everyone smiled because, as I remembered, Aunt Netty was Grandma Tessy's own daughter. I thought she must be very worried about her mother being sick for so long.

Mrs. Hauser came back with Grandma Tessy's plate, saying, "Just a small slice of ham and a little more white meat—no skin—and some dressing with a spoonful of piccalilli, please."

Aunt Netty got up, saying she thought she had heard Kenny crying. Martha, sitting next to Fran, said something to Mother about Grandma Tessy that I didn't catch after Aunt Netty had left.

Uncle Drew said, "We must never forget to be mannerly," in a way that sounded almost as if he meant to be funny.

Aunt Harriet asked in a slightly teasing tone, "Just how many servants do you have in Shanghai, Emma?"

Mother flushed. "It's hard to give an accurate picture. Supervising people is often more difficult than doing something yourself."

Uncle Drew looked at me. "Pass your plate, Tom, we've got to feed you up."

"I wouldn't want to keep anyone else from having more," I said, really trying to make a joke this time, because there was a lot of turkey left and at least half the ham. Mrs. Hauser had refilled the vegetable dishes and the gravy boat for the mashed potatoes.

I was rewarded by laughter, so I said, "I thought that would entertain you."

Heidi Hauser made a face at Martha, but Martha smiled at me and Rob whispered, "Atta boy, Tom!" Uncle Drew grinned, but I heard Uncle Fred mutter under his breath, "Entertain—what a word!" Aunt Harriet turned over a piece of ham on her plate and attacked it with her fork. Fran winked at me, so that was all right.

Aunt Louise and Aunt Harriet and Mother began helping Mrs. Hauser remove the dinner plates.

Mrs. Hauser came back with dessert plates of hot apple pie, the home-churned vanilla ice-cream melting on it. Everyone looked hot to me. Uncle Drew and Uncle Fred loosened their belts without even trying to make it look as if they were doing something else. I oozed all over and felt sleepy, but then Grandma Tessy's cane hit the floor again and Mrs. Hauser said, "I'm sure she'd like a little ice cream at least."

When the women started to clear the table, the men looked at each other and smiled. Rob and Brooks stood up with me and Brooks said, "Let's go out back and loosen up with a game of horseshoes. You ever pitch horseshoes, Tom?"

"No," I said. "Is it hard to learn?"

"I wouldn't say it is," Brooks said. "In fact, offhand I can't think of anyone who couldn't at least grasp the theory of horseshoes."

We followed Uncle Drew and Uncle Fred into the back yard past the old outhouse and the barn that had been turned first into a carriage house and then a garage.

As we stepped inside it all I could see at first in the shadows was a big heap of corn cobs, but as my eyes got used to the dark while

Brooks was getting horseshoes off a nail near the side door I saw a big black touring car behind the stack of cobs. A layer of dust covered it, but I could read LIBERTY on the red-white-and-blue nameplate.

"That looks like a powerful car," I said.

"It is," Brooks said. "Grandfather hasn't used it much lately, so it's in bad shape. We want Dad to let us fix it so they can sell it."

"Can you fix a car?" I asked in some awe.

"Sure thing," Rob said.

"I suppose it can go really quite fast," I said.

"Not bad," Brooks said.

"Do you suppose it could do sixty?" I asked.

"Sixty!" Brooks exclaimed. "Sixty, he asks!"

"I know that's terribly fast," I said.

"Oh, *terribly, terribly* fast *indeed!*" Brooks said. "That's a Liberty Six and it can do a *hundred* when it's really tuned up."

Uncle Drew and Uncle Fred laughed, leaving me wondering if the Liberty Six really could do anything like a hundred or even sixty as I followed Brooks and Rob outside.

The stakes for the horseshoes had been driven in along the side facing the house, each in a dusty cup. "We ought to move them," Rob said. "It gets too easy."

"Sure, but not right now," Brooks said. "They'll give Tom a bit of help." He showed me how to hold the horseshoe and pitch it, sending the shoe circling flat on itself with an arm swing across his body from left to right. The shoe hit the stake and kicked over, landing in a puff of dust on the far rim of the cup.

"There's another way," he said, "that seems easier at first, but if you miss the flip it can really kick back." He sent the second shoe turning directly over on itself, his arm coming straight up beside his body as he took a single step to the line.

The shoe ringed the stake and I said, "I'll try that way first."

"You shouldn't have shown him that," Rob protested. "It's never as good as the other way unless you practice and practice, and even then . . . "

"Oh, who cares?" Brooks interrupted.

I sent a shoe sailing way over the stake. I got a little better as I went on, and I tried the first motion, but my aim seemed much worse that way. Rob kept fretting about not starting me off right and Brooks teased him. Then Rob said, "You ought to think about it, because what will the guys say, especially fat old Bert Kratz and Rusty Blair, when they see our Chinese cousin pitching horseshoes that showoff way?"

Brooks stopped teasing. "Maybe you're right. Tom, please try it the regular way again."

My aim was still wild. Brooks said, "Tom could always say that's the way they pitch in China."

"Listen," Rob said, "you've got to remember what it's like for us right now."

Brooks nodded. "Please try it again the real right way, Tom," he said in his normal voice.

Rob had walked to the first stake and pitched the four shoes back in jig time.

I tried it again, and though I got closer it was still a wild pitch. I took the second shoe and that was no better. The third went even wider. With the fourth shoe I tried the easier, showoff way and as I sailed it in a higher arc than before, the sunlight caught the turning metal, burnished by all those landings in the dust, and there it flashed coming down beautifully, turning perfectly, and clinking against the stake as it chunked down in an explosion of dust—a ringer.

"Good man!" Rob called out. Brooks clapped. "If it goes like that most of the time, we can quit worrying. And anyway, we're all Lloyds together in this, aren't we?"

That was a pretty keen thing for him to say because I was just as much a Jerome as a Lloyd.

"That's for sure," Rob said, and that was pretty keen, too, because I knew he couldn't be crazy about having a skinny younger cousin from China hanging around who didn't talk or dress quite right. I felt a kind of sweaty love for them both.

Uncle Drew and Uncle Fred had come out around the far corner of the barn and stood in the shadow of what I guessed was a stand of locust trees, its shadow so deep in that sunlight that I hadn't noticed them earlier. My eye caught a movement of Uncle Drew's right hand. I grinned to myself, thinking he had already forgotten about hiding his cigar from me. At the same time I said, "I'll keep working at pitching, and that seems the right way for me," when I saw he wasn't smoking but passing a flat brown bottle over to Uncle Fred. I thought of explaining "moonshine" to Fran.

We never pitched a real game that afternoon, but I kept getting better. Uncle Drew and Uncle Fred went back into the barn for a while and when they came out Uncle Drew said, "Well, gentlemen, now that the ladies must have finished we should go in and offer our help before we see if it isn't time to leave."

Rob carried the horseshoes into the barn. At the kitchen door, Rob caught up with us. He put his hands under my armpits and swung me up the steps. "You really are a lightweight, aren't you?"

"I've always been skinny," I said.

Brooks turned at that and said, "I used to be, too, but never let anybody call you skinny, or if they do, just say you prefer to be *slim*. That stops them every time!"

I liked that.

After the others had left, Mother came up to me and said, "Tom, I think we should have a little talk."

Fran heard her and asked, "May I come too?"

"Yes," Mother said. "We could go out on the back steps."

She took off the faded blue apron she'd been wearing.

Fran and I sat on the bottom step looking up at Mother.

"I'm learning to pitch horseshoes," I said.

Fran said, "I suppose that's part of what you want to talk about, Mother, isn't it?"

"Yes, it is," Mother said, and I felt nettled. "I think, Tom, you may have forgotten what day it is." Her tone was mild.

Then I saw it—it was the Sabbath. "I forgot," I said. "Brooks and Rob were with me and Uncle Drew and Uncle Fred saw us too, even if they spent some time in the barn where they were . . . looking at Grandfather's Liberty Six," I ended abruptly.

"I know," Mother said. "It *is* different, and I'm not sure what we should do. I don't know what your father would say."

"He wouldn't like it," Fran said.

That was too much, even from Fran. What I knew was a divinely inspired question came to me. "Would Grandfather Lloyd have pitched horseshoes on Sunday?"

Taken unawares, Mother smiled. "Oh, Papa always enjoyed all kinds of games on Sundays when he could relax and forget about the bank."

And there she was trapped, and Fran was trapped, and I kept my face in the worried expression it had taken on at the thought of whether I had sinned and what Father might think, but I could feel the inner laughter pulsing through me. Neither Mother nor Fran said anything and we sat there in our private worlds until I finally said, "I wonder which way Grandfather Lloyd pitched horseshoes."

6

AND THERE it was. I tried to persuade myself that "the quivering glimmer of sun and rill with a sudden flash on the eye was thrown," but it was nothing like that. I saw a bridge and knew what it spanned. I pulled off onto the shoulder, got out, and walked to the middle of the bridge. Muddy, slightly roiled water flowed under me. I had nursed a wan hope that it might be some shade of green, but I knew I shouldn't expect that, having learned years before that it was named after a man and not for its color.

Back in the Chevy, I drove across the bridge and into Green River, Utah. At a market I bought some cold cuts and a half-pint carton of milk, eating an early lunch in the car. After I'd eaten I sat there for a few minutes, thinking that nothing made this place any different from dozens of other towns. Not much to ponder; so I started the motor and drove on through.

The immediate landscape looked dull. The snow-covered mountains to the north and the stretches of desert to the south showed some character, but right here along the road everything seemed ordinary enough.

I felt a loss of momentum. Only the boyhood anticipation of crossing a border, heading into another state, urged me towards the Colorado line. Then the old charm began to work—either that, or I imagined a lift in the road. Most satisfying of all as I crossed the line and headed for Mack and Fruita—splendid names—was knowing that I approached the road that Father would least approve of: a truly secondary—tertiary?—one running almost due north from Fruita to Rangely with nothing in between. I almost regretted that he would approve of my stopping to make sure I set out on that road with a full tank of gas.

The snow patches stayed about the same size, and when I reached a filling station in Fruita I decided to risk going on without asking questions. But as I walked back from the men's room, the attendant looked at me and asked, "Why in hell don't you go back to where it's warm?"

"Nothing like a little change," I said.

"I wouldn't mind one, for sure. I suppose you're heading for Denver?"

"No, I'm heading north to Rangely and on to Vernon."

"Who would want to go there?"

"I'm really going beyond."

"Oh well," he said. "I suppose you plan to rent skis and all that?"

"No, I'm no skier."

"I thought you must be hitting it up for Steamboat Springs."

"I'm heading up to Wyoming," I said.

"It's your choice."

"Right," I said, frowning as I pocketed my credit card. This had gone on long enough. "It's on family business, of course."

"That's different," he said. "You may hit some snow. You got chains?"

"Sure thing."

"Good," he said. "And good luck."

"Thanks, buddy," I signed off.

Heading north, I came to bleak hillsides, dotted with snow and dead grass streaked by rivulets. I felt enough confidence in my hard-won mastery of American patterns to believe that it would have been the attendant's duty to speak out if he knew the road was impassable.

I took about an hour to get to Rangely, where I turned west on much the same kind of road, heading for Vernal, and that took perhaps half an hour. At Vernal, the mountains ahead showed themselves real mountains. I drove through a modest residential section. A short distance out of town my county-numbered road circled and began to climb. As I swung around and above a small valley I saw a marsh hawk gliding below me, the white at the base of its tail sooty against the snow.

The patches joined to form a field of snow broken here and there by the shelter of scrub. The names on wooden markers began a slow chime—Sheep Creek Bay, Henry's Fork, Anvil Draw. Trying to arrange them in their own rhythm, I failed to catch all of a sign starting with Buckboard. I thought of backing, but that wasn't in the pattern, so I went on, forever ignorant of what kind of Buckboard it was, past signs to Black's Fork and Lost Dog. Lost dog, indeed! On and on until I was climbing to the top of the world.

Below and to my right I caught sight of the upper cliffs of the Flaming Gorge. Far below, the river, my river, must be boiling down through rocky chutes.

When I saw another vehicle approaching, a pickup, I came close to feeling my privacy violated. I pulled over to let it pass. Coming alongside, the driver waved, smiling, the ear flaps of his fur cap pulled down. I waved back, knowing that I showed just the right degree of solidarity and friendliness—the wordless salute of two adventurers out in the wilds.

Now I climbed the real heights and had to ease carefully across icy stretches. The pickup hadn't had chains on, which was a good sign, unless the driver was just a local man. Just a local man—was that what I didn't want to be? I felt I should be back in California if I was going to think this way, because there, in that society built for the automobile, solitary driving is a kind of meditation, a consultation with oneself. Perhaps this was part of being a Westerner, a solitary, meditative driver through life. I'd tried to explain this years ago to Eastern friends. In the face of total puzzlement, even suspicion of my sanity, I'd given up after a couple of tries.

A second vehicle approached, taking the curves with the teetering caution of a top-heavy camper. I saw the Indiana license plate. This time *I* was the one to wave and smile first. The middle-aged couple on the front seat responded with worried looks and a shake of the driver's head.

I felt let down, thinking there had to be something important about the Hoosier camper. Then it came to me—chains. Something truly important to think about, I told myself, mocking my meditative mood. As if I didn't have enough to think about as it was, trying to live in the illusion of a private world both secret and expansive, like those worlds of my youth.

That simple dualism—surely the basis of all error in the other kind of Western thought—hadn't had to be revised in Dalton. I knew now that the issues requiring those revisions remained the grand old Puritan centers of money and sex. Here I was on my way to Dalton by way of Wyoming because of money, certainly— but sex?

My first not too serious blunder in Dalton came, I had to admit, from what one would have to call sex. Mother had been left in charge of the infant Kenny one afternoon. When he woke, Mother brought him down into the kitchen.

"He's certainly soaked!" she exclaimed as she spread out a receiving blanket on the kitchen table. She unpinned his diaper, washed, dried, and powdered him while I stood at a little distance. She slid a fresh diaper under him and just as she was ready to fold it over, Kenny produced what could only be called a minor erection, though I had no English for it at that age.

"Oh dear!" Mother said. "He's going to wet again. I'll have to start all over."

"It doesn't have to mean that," I remarked, not thinking of what I was saying. I hadn't been particularly struck by Kenny's performance, and I'm not sure that even in Shanghai I wouldn't have confused my worlds.

"What's that?" Mother asked sharply.

"I beg your pardon?"

"What else *could* it mean?" she demanded.

"Oh, I don't know," I said, in full retreat. "Nothing, I guess. I just meant I wasn't sure he would have to wet again so soon."

"But *could* it mean something else?" she persisted.

"I beg your pardon?" I said again, thinking of the genial patting I sometimes got from the cook or the table boy in an exchange of casual favors that never went farther than that.

"Now, Tom," Mother said, "you heard me perfectly well. Sometimes I think you say 'I beg your pardon?' just to annoy people."

"I don't want to annoy anyone," I said. "I'm sorry, it's just that Father doesn't think I should say 'What?' the way most people do."

Mother looked exasperated. Kenny didn't wet before he subsided, which may have annoyed her further. "You really haven't answered my question," she insisted.

I had had time to recover by now. "I'm afraid I didn't understand it," I said. "I meant that I wasn't sure Kenny would wet again, and he hasn't. What did you think I was saying?"

I knew I had my most innocent, puzzled, even slightly hurt expression on my face by now. Mother looked at me suspiciously as I patted Kenny's cheek and gave him my right index finger to hold. I knew that was almost a challenge, but I kept my face the same and she gave it up, turning to get his bottle ready.

This dim sense of sexuality kept me from saying anything about babies to Fran, but I did remark to her that our relatives seemed to do a lot of things themselves that we expected our servants to do in China.

She said loftily, "Oh yes, surely you know that we're straight middle class, maybe just a little bit upper."

"What's that?"

"What we are," she said, not very helpfully.

"Well, I don't really mind," I said. "But I didn't expect it."

"Of course there's Mrs. Hauser," she said.

"I know."

"And of course I remember what it was like from before."

I couldn't help thinking that for all her offers to explain things to me, Fran had never said a word about this.

"If they had a hired girl or a hired man, he or she would live with them," she said.

"Yes, but it isn't the same thing," I protested.

So there it was: the money was turning out to be not much money after all, and in Dalton the sex remained a half-realized force.

I had to give up on this because the road called for attention. After crossing a couple of short ice-covered stretches, I knew I must get out the chains. I couldn't remember exactly how long it had been since I'd used them. On our annual winter jaunts into the San Gabriels to build a snowman with Mary and Maude, Amy and I drove to the first clear stretch of snow and stopped. When we left, after eating a picnic lunch and playing around for a while, I always felt I was betraying the white figure we had created, abandoning him there to the elements. I thought I might be making this trip as a penance, as well as to see if I couldn't break out of a few constrictions.

I pulled into a narrow turnout, shivering as the cold hit me when I opened the car door, and clumsily draped the chains over the rear tires, ready to roll forward. The right chain slipped off on my first try. I secured the left one and backed up to start over. By the time I'd finished, my fingers ached and I put them in my mouth for a while before going on.

I knew I must be nearing the pass, the high point between my Green Rivers. There it was at last, a small marker: SUMMIT. I pulled over again, the chains biting into crusted snow. I took out a plastic tumbler from my things in the Chevy's trunk and packed it half full of snow, then topped it off with what was left of the fifth of Teacher's.

At first I felt too inhibited to try any kind of toast except for an unvoiced one to all the Green Rivers of my life. I took a good swallow, the snow adding a not unpleasant, earthy taste to the scotch.

"Not unpleasant, indeed!" I startled myself by proclaiming aloud. Before I took my next swallow I raised the tumbler to the sky and offered, "To the double negative!"

That was the right way to handle it.

"Hitting the road" hardly described my cautious swinging of the Chevy back into the snow-filled ruts and letting the chains take hold, feeling the pull of the motor and the slight lag in steering. Whenever I struck an icy bit I could hear the slapslap of the chains and moused along carefully, knowing the river was off there to the east. I would soon be entering Wyoming, the state of the mystic acres that probably weren't worth a cent more than Mr. Kneller was paying for them.

I came down from the mountains, sliding out on the curves. Now and then I caught sight of the gorge's upper cliffs. Then the road swung away from them, below the level of snow and ice. At last I came into Green River, Wyoming. Crossing the river, I felt in the evening light that it really showed a dull slaty green shade between the ice-encrusted banks. In the central district near the railroad station I saw a hotel that looked so much a part of the past that I knew I must put up there.

The main street itself appeared impossibly Western. I wondered if I had missed something at the other Green River, after all, but I knew I hadn't. Here the fronts of the business establishments looked as if they might be the original fronts, so authentic that they might be false, which was what they would be anyway. I pulled into a parking space about twenty feet from the hotel entrance. A switching engine whistled somewhere down the line. At the desk, the clerk pushed a form in front of me and said, "Where from today?"

"Salina," I said, "up through the other Green River and on here over the mountains."

"It's a good thing you had chains." He sounded respectful.

"How did you know?" I asked.

"Hell, man, I could hear you coming for a couple of blocks. You may get a citation for tearing up the pavement."

"I'm afraid I didn't think about that."

"Just kidding," he said.

"I'm too tired to take them off, anyway," I said. "And I'm a touch high on scotch."

"Only way to go," he said.

"One way, at least," I said. I carried my things to the shabby room right down the hall on the first floor, following the clerk, who unlocked the door for me.

"Any place to get a bite?"

"Coffee shop on the next corner," he said.

"And a drink?"

"A bar two blocks down, or a bottle shop halfway into the block from the coffee shop."

I walked to the liquor store and picked up a fifth of Teacher's.

Back in my room, I poured two fingers into a tumbler and, after kicking off my shoes, stretched out on the bed.

Not too many miles to the northeast lay the Wyoming acreage. Tomorrow I would become the first descendant of Thomas Drew Lloyd to look at the piece of land that had held his heirs in thrall. I would start the process of release, almost as if I were ransoming all of us. I would go on to Dalton and later take the papers to the Center City probate court. And that would be that.

Green River to Green River, with a tumbler of scotch in your hand and your feet up on the folded blanket of a bed in an old hotel, thinking in double negatives. Whatever it meant wouldn't be revealed with a flash of lightning and a clap of thunder.

When the glass showed empty, I swung my legs over the side of the bed, groped for my shoes with my toes and got up. I took my appointment book from my briefcase and went back down the hall to the desk, where I asked the clerk how I could put through a phone call.

"Come around here and use the switchboard," he said. "We're so antique and authentic that we've never put in room extensions. The owner's afraid we might raise the tone of the place beyond its usefulness." I looked at him hard. "It's just that a place like this can make a decent profit as long as it doesn't change too much, because the newer places need it for comparison."

"An interesting view," I ventured.

"Fairly, if it isn't too obvious," he said.

"I can't say it would have been obvious to me," I said.

"That's generous of you," he said. "What's the number you want to reach?"

I found Mr. Kneller's number and gave it to him. "Take a seat," he said, indicating a swivel chair beside the switchboard.

"Any special name?" he asked.

"Whoever answers," I said.

He rang up the exchange and after some time he handed me a receiver. "Hello?" I heard a man's voice saying.

"Hello," I said. "Is this Mr. George Kneller?"

"That's right," the voice, standard, rather flat, answered.

"This is Tom Jerome calling from Green River," I said. "You know, I'm bringing along the papers to close everything on that property in my grandfather's estate and I'd like to see you tomorrow."

"Mr. Thomas Jerome! You mean you got as far as Green River and stopped, instead of coming straight on through to us?"

"I've had quite a day," I said. "I've driven from Salina in Utah through Green River on that side to Green River here," I said.

"At this time of year?"

"It seemed an interesting exercise," I said lamely, feeling as if I had exposed myself not only to Mr. Kneller but also to the man at the desk.

After a pause, Mr. Kneller asked, "Is everyone in your family—well, a bit eccentric?" He forced a laugh.

"You could say that," I said.

"I can believe it," he said. "But look, Mr. Jerome, get a good start in the morning and we'll expect you for lunch. I'll have everything ready, notary and all. And of course you'll spend a few days with us."

"Oh, I'm afraid that's too much to ask of you," I said.

"Listen, Mr. Jerome, after all these years to see in the flesh a member of the Lloyd family isn't something to take casually. My two sons and my daughter are all coming in, not so much for this as for a kind of family party—near my birthday, you know."

"I'm only half Lloyd," I said, "but I can assure you that the Jeromes are in their own way quite as eccentric as their in-laws."

He didn't know how to take that, I thought, because he cleared his throat before answering. After all, he had started this, so I waited. "That's very interesting," he said finally, "but now let me tell you exactly how to get here. I hope you're not just a city driver, expecting smooth pavement all the way."

"No," I said. "I believe I just said that I've come from Green River to Green River."

"Of course," he said. "Sorry—it's such a crazy thing to do at this time of year that I'd almost refused to believe you. I mean, I haven't quite taken it in."

"That's all right," I said. "I can drive any road, so don't fret. Just give me clear directions, and please don't say about any particular turn-off or landmark that I can't possibly miss it."

This earned a respectful snort. "I see what you mean about both your families." He told me where to turn off a little before Latham, and gave me the series of back roads that would bring me to what he literally called his "spread." Never before had I heard that term used seriously in ordinary conversation. Driving from Green River to Green River had brought me something new, after all.

When I'd hung up, the clerk said, "That was old George Kneller, the stock man, wasn't it?"

"Right. You know him?" I hoped to pick up some item of striking information to report back to Pasadena, just to show that I had done my inadequate best.

"I come from near Latham," he said, "or at least my folks did. Almost anyone around here would know who George Kneller is. He's a very solid citizen."

"I see."

"You planning on buying some stock? Funny time of year for buying stock, if you don't mind my saying so."

"No, hardly," I said, dazzled by a vision of myself in a sweat-stained Stetson, starting a drive through the mountains with a hundred head of cattle and a motley crew of cowhands.

"I didn't think you looked the type."

"Thanks. Actually, I'm going to sell Mr. Kneller something, you could say."

"So you're a salesman? You'll find George Kneller no easy mark."

"I'm sure he isn't," I said. "But I'm not a salesman. I'm a professor of English."

"Christ!" he said automatically.

I wondered what would reduce him to total silence but decided it wasn't worth it. "It's just some family property he leases and is planning to buy."

That brought him back to the straight and narrow. "Good grazing land up there."

"So they say. I don't suppose there's anything else is there?" I tried to admire my astuteness through Mother's eyes.

"Not that I know of," he said. "Of course nowadays people do some prospecting, looking for new minerals and that kind of stuff."

"I suppose."

"No strikes anywhere near there that I've heard of. Nice part of the state. I guess you've seen it if you own land."

"Not right there," I said. "This was my grandfather's investment—part of his estate."

"They always say land is good to hold onto."

"So they do, but there isn't enough of this to make much out of, considering the number of heirs."

"A long probate?"

"Something over twenty years," I said. He whistled. "Hard to get everyone in a family to agree," I said and he nodded.

Driving down to the coffee shop I heard the chains on the Chevy. I turned into a filling station and asked how late they were open.

"Forever," the attendant said. "This is a through highway and even in this season we pick up some night jobs."

I arranged to have the chains taken off and the car serviced.

At the coffee shop I sat at the counter and ordered a rare T-bone.

Back at the hotel, I said goodnight to the clerk, even though he acted as if he'd been waiting for me and might want to go on talking.

"It's been a long day," I said. "Maybe I'll see you in the morning."

"That's not impossible."

I went right to bed after pouring myself a nightcap. I lay there sipping the scotch and thinking about what the clerk had said about the building being needed in its way. I thought what George Kneller's voice had sounded like and how he had picked up on my remark about not saying I couldn't miss the way.

I drifted for a time, and then, afraid of falling asleep with the glass in my hand, I finished it off, set the tumbler down, turned over on my left side, and went to sleep.

7 🐚

Measured on the national standard for that kind of thing, Mr. Kneller's instructions for reaching his place rated a B+. He had twice miscounted the number of intersections to be passed, but on our family tours I had picked up the knack of ignoring anything that a local person might call a "lane."

Once I'd reached the turn-off a little before Latham, the Chevy climbed at a steady rate until I came to the top of a rise. Here the road leveled off and I looked out over an expanse of rolling land. The road ran along the other side in a gentle descent to the northeast before curving down across the slope. An occasional mailbox stood at the junction of the main road and a private road leading back into the hills. I had a considerable distance to go still, but I looked at the names anyway—Carter, Pritchard, Eaton, Benton, MacIntosh—all bland enough.

The outsize box with KNELLER on it announced a family of substance. The private, paved "lane" looked in good repair. Whereas I had been able to catch a glimpse of buildings from time to time at the other turn-offs, here I knew I had a couple of miles still to go. The lane curved through rounded foothills, then came into the open again on the edge of a small cup valley, the kind of private retreat that made me think of the never-never-lands that Zane Grey wrote of—the hidden valley that could be cut off from the rest of the world forever by toppling over the Balancing Rock. I couldn't believe the Knellers wanted that sort of Edenic isolation. The first out-buildings I came on told a history of solid development: smaller structures at one side of holding corrals, a few old trees, and the newer house on the other side, built in a squat H shape.

A shallow curved driveway brought me to the entrance. I pulled up, aware of the storm door opening as I got out and saw what must be George Kneller coming down the steps.

I had cherished an inner image of a bluff, hearty Western rancher. He was sparer than I had expected, and shorter, a bit younger than Father, and that surprised me.

He held out his hand and we greeted each other. He made no more than a ritual protest when I refused to let him take my bag and briefcase. In the house I felt a sense of solid comfort, of living in a way that went with the land.

"I'll show you to your room," he said, leading me through the main hallway and turning into one of the wings. "If you want to wash up, say so," he went on as he opened the door to a motel-like bedroom, "but if not, or if you make it fast, just put your things down here. My old lady is busy and we could have a quick one. Most of the family is coming this afternoon. We all hope you'll stay the night."

"I'm afraid that's putting you out," I said, "especially when you have a full house."

"Nothing to it," he said. "We're used to crowds, and in the winter we can use the old place's extra rooms and even the bunk-house."

He sounded sincere, and I chided myself for trying to hear some kind of false heartiness in his speech. It was just that it cut so close to the public image of that kind of thing that, like the buildings in Green River, a false front was the true front, and perhaps George Kneller had no front at all.

That came close to putting me off. I knew I had my own front, and I felt disarmed. Not that there had to be anything like a contest between us since Aunt Netty and the other heirs had yielded.

He showed me into his office, a masculine, leather-furnished den, with nothing in the way of books but a shelf of ledgers.

Opening a cabinet bar, he asked, "What's for you?"

JOHN ESPEY

"Scotch, neat, please," I said.

"Aha," he said, "the Eastern taste."

"There's nothing Eastern about me," I said, "unless you're talking globally."

"East of here at least," he insisted.

"Hardly, except for a couple of summers."

"Now I remember," he said. "You're from the Chinese branch."

"Right."

After he handed me my glass he poured about three fingers of Four Roses into his, dropped in some ice cubes, and added a little soda water. "Well then, gung ho!" he said, lifting his drink.

Taken off-guard, I heard myself saying "Bottoms up!" in the Shanghai dialect. "I ran into someone from around Latham who knows you—the desk clerk in the Green River Hotel."

"That would be Paul Keaton," he said. "He's something of a local character."

"That's what he said about you."

"Not in the same way, though," he said. "Paul always has theories about things."

"And you?"

"I'm not what you'd call a thinker, Mr. Jerome."

"Do call me Tom," I said.

"Glad to," he said. "I just take hold of whatever seems to be coming around the corner next and don't worry about it. But with Paul Keaton—funny you should call him the desk clerk. One of his acts, you know."

"Acts?"

"In a way," he said, taking a good pull of his drink. "He *is* the desk clerk a lot of the time—says it gives him a feeling of what's going on in the world. But whether or not he's the desk clerk at any particular time, he's always the owner of the property. Won't even consider what might seem an unreasonably high offer for the place."

"I suppose I should have guessed," I said.

"Good thing you didn't—he'd have felt embarrassed," he said. "Funny having a part Lloyd here at last. I don't know how many letters, how many messages have gone between the Lloyds and me since your grandfather—it *was* your grandfather, wasn't it, Tom?—died. I guess it's been a matter of stubbornness and family feeling on both sides."

"I'm sure you're right," I said. "Sometimes I think I've spent my whole life with the Wyoming acreage. I kept hearing about it again and again after I spent that first summer in Dalton."

"Dalton!" he said, raising his glass again. "So you've actually been to Dalton?"

"Yes," I said. "This trip is a kind of the return of the non-native for me, because there's one thing I don't have—a real American home town, though I suppose I keep pretending that's what Dalton is."

"What kind of place is it really?"

"That's part of what I'm trying to find out on this trip," I said. Then, thinking that might sound too cryptic, I said, "What I mean is that I keep trying to find out what Dalton is for me personally."

He looked contented enough as he sipped his Four Roses again, and I took another swallow of my scotch—not Teacher's, but Old Rarity. I wondered if all brands of scotch were named in a sort of open symbolism.

Then I realized Mr. Kneller was waiting for me to go on, so I said, "What I mean is that Dalton stands for a lot of things to me that it probably wouldn't to anyone else. It's probably no different from dozens of other small towns in the Middle West."

I had supposed, from what he had said, that Mr. Kneller and I were sneaking our drinks before lunch in a masculine conspiracy, so when the office opened and a woman said, "Well, George, you might at least have brought our guest to say hello to me, but I guess you thought I was too busy," I assumed we had been found out.

I had jumped up and Mrs. Kneller and I met midway and shook hands. Her face showed weathering and she had a firm grip. "I hope that George has at least shown you to your room."

"Oh, yes," I said.

George Kneller showed no embarrassment, simply getting up to fix what must be his wife's regular drink, Four Roses over ice.

"I'm afraid I'm really putting you out," I said, after we'd all raised glasses.

"Not at all," Mrs. Kneller said. "We built this new place when the children were still with us, so we rattle around a bit now. You know, it's hard to believe that this endless business is finally getting settled."

"Yes," I said. "I feel a bit silly about my part in it, though. I'm sure everyone knows as well as I do that the whole thing could have been wound up courtesy of the U.S. Post Office. But it gave me a good excuse for a short holiday that everyone insists I stand in need of. And I've loved to drive ever since I was a boy, and there's always been a feeling that some member of the family, even one like me out on the fringe, should actually look at what we've called 'the Wyoming acreage' ever since I can remember."

"You really want to see it?" George Kneller asked.

"If that can be managed at this time of year," I said. "I can't imagine being here and not looking at it."

"It'll be a rough ride, but we can make it in the Jeep. How about tomorrow morning after breakfast?"

"Fine," I said, knowing that I had committed myself to spending the night, something I hadn't been sure I wanted to do, as if this pause might be too great an interruption in my reverse crossing of the land.

A car horn gave two long blasts followed by a shorter one somewhere near us.

"Why, that's Junior!" Mrs. Kneller exclaimed. "I wasn't expecting them until after lunch. Isn't this nice?"

She sounded perfectly sincere, as if it were the most natural thing in the world for Junior and his family to arrive early for an unplanned lunch. I thought of what this kind of irregularity would produce back at the Elizabeth Street household, or indeed, at Amy's and mine. On the other hand, no one would ever be called Junior at either place.

And now laughter broke out as Junior and his wife and their two children joined us. They were all sweatered, with what looked like Scandinavian patterns front and back—antlered animal heads—and the room became overpoweringly active. Mr. and Mrs. Kneller were introducing me and mixing drinks and greeting their grandchildren all at the same time. I wondered if it hadn't been something like this in Dalton long ago with Grandfather Lloyd still alive, the center of a big family, interested in them all and pronouncing his dicta.

Not that George Kneller sounded all that dogmatic about anything, but I could see that he enjoyed this, that it was all part of success to him, just as, I suspected, my being there was also part of success. Though Junior and his wife, Gladys, spoke warmly to me and the children shook hands, I couldn't help feeling very much the foreigner.

At least I felt that way until Junior, glass in hand—they all drank Four Roses—said, "It's great to meet you, Mr. Lloyd—I mean Jerome, of course—I keep forgetting because we call that section of grazing land the Lloyd section, you know—and I know Gladys will want to talk to you about the things you've written about growing up in China."

"You don't say?" I had uttered one of Father's set phrases, one he used to give himself time to adjust his views on discovering something he hadn't anticipated.

"Yes," Junior said, and called across the room. "Gladys, you must tell Mr. Jerome about reading his stuff."

Which was all right and placed Junior pretty well, especially when Gladys came over and said, "Now, Junebug, you've given me away."

Junebug was so ludicrous a nickname for this solid-chested all-American citizen that my left eyebrow shot up in spite of myself. I tried to get it down without grimacing, but even as I went through this absurd exercise I thought how unnecessary it was. A lifted eyebrow among the Knellers was a non-existent act. Only Gladys, I thought, might notice, but this seemed unlikely when she said, "Actually, you don't look very Chinese, Mr. Jerome."

"Do call me Tom, please," I said. "I'm afraid I've disappointed you, Mrs. Kneller."

"Oh, don't say that, and please call me Gladys," she said. "You know we're all just plain folks here in the West. I know it was a stupid remark, because you aren't Chinese at all, are you, but somehow . . . "

"I used to be taken for a Eurasian sometimes when I was a kid," I said. "With my dark hair and eyes it looked more probable than it may now. I think the mustache pretty well kills all that, don't you?"

"It's very exotic," Gladys said. I could see that it really was, that I stood for something in their minds quite unlike anything that I stood for in my own.

We put down a second round of drinks before Mrs. Kneller said, "I think lunch is ready, but you'll be taking pot luck because I hadn't planned for quite so many."

We trooped into a sunny dining room in the central section of the house. And there I was, back in a big family party, and back in Dalton too, in my mind, thinking how strange it was to be part of this. Not that we didn't sit down as a family with my parents in Pasadena, but that was a ritual affair, where only one person spoke at a time. Here everyone talked, even the children, and if I was an exotic, I managed to fit in fairly well because sitting on Mrs. Kneller's right I might as well be beside Aunt Louise or Aunt Netty, chatting about the weather, the food, having some of her own preserves pressed on me, and the table with its profusion of side dishes reminded me of Dalton too.

I soon understood that Mrs. Kneller hadn't produced all this by waving a wand. Two girls in their teens came in to help, and I had a vision of what the family table at Dalton might have grown into through the years if that unit had survived and prospered instead of breaking up.

My train of thought was derailed when Junebug spoke across the table to me. "Dad says you're a wild driver, ready to tackle any snowbound track. You know, we get so many drivers from the Midwest who have a heart attack as soon as they hit the mountains."

"Oh, I don't know," I said, feeling exposed, and wondering if I should say anything about why I had gone through that particular passage. I decided that since the Knellers were at last getting the

Wyoming acreage from us I needn't give them anything more, so I went on, "Actually, my wife, Amy, makes fun of my driving. She's a Hollywood girl, you know, and she claims that ever since a particular road in the San Gabriel Mountains has been closed, crosscountry driving has lost its challenge."

Junebug's attention had been caught by the mention of Hollywood. I could see that that, too, was something exotic here at the Kneller table. "You mean your wife is . . . " he started, and I interrupted with "A graduate of Hollywood High. If she were here she'd be happy to tell you how Charlie Chaplin once patted her grandmother on the head and said she'd be ideal for a part in one of his films. But her grandmother was the widow of a Presbyterian missionary to the Mormons and told him as politely as she could that he had 'mistaken her character.' "

Junebug was completely at sea by now and I had to admit that what I had said, though perfectly accurate, must sound just this side of insane. So I did my best to rescue him by adding, "That was long ago, you know. The place has gone downhill badly since then."

"Is that so?" he managed to get out and I said, "Yes," and we made our escape by discussing the various techniques of putting on chains.

At the end of the meal Mrs. Kneller, whom by this time I was calling Grace, said, "You must make yourself completely at home, Tom."

"I'm a bit tired from the drive," I said. "Perhaps I'll stretch out for a while."

In my room I took off my shoes and propped myself up on the bed. I just wanted to get away for a moment by myself. Thinking about the Knellers and my own family reminded me that Mother had said Amy was generous to let me go on this trip alone. I wasn't sure that that was true. Amy and I had reached a point in our marriage that must bring questions to us both, what with the ordinary pressures of our two daughters, the sheer dailiness of life, the settled patterns.

I wondered sometimes if Amy ever asked herself, as I did, if we were at a particular given time "doing whichever you'd rather." Sometimes I felt we were doing exactly as we'd been told to do by someone else.

It wasn't a bad plan, and since we had both been told pretty much the same things, we usually agreed. At first I thought this was intimacy, but I had begun to wonder, and I suspected that Amy, too, was wondering. Amy had wanted more than two children because she had been an unhappy, unwanted, only child, and the book said that a child needs companionship. That was fine with me. Certainly I would never have survived without Fran. But then Amy had problems with her second pregnancy, and after all, the book said that two children ideally fitted our station in life.

We rubbed along pretty well in bed and out, so I wondered how generous Amy was being. I had proposed that we make a winter family tour of it all, but she had shied off from the very first. And I had to admit that the sheer logistics were daunting. We had enough trouble making our ritual visits to Pasadena.

That both our children were girls pleased Amy enormously. I found that I had no carry-over from the back of the house in Shanghai on that score. I felt no regret until Amy explained to me in an unusual burst of direct speech not only why she was happy to have two daughters but thought it best, everything considered, that we had no son.

"I can't imagine you, Tom," she said, "getting out with a ball and bat or playing touch football in the park, or doing any of those things to provide a model for a red-blooded, all-American boy to follow. Anyway, I suspect I wouldn't be comfortable with a boy around all the time."

"I've taught the girls to ride their bikes," I said.

"Yes, and I'm glad you have."

To find Amy thus almost in league with my parents and the rest of my relatives rankled.

"There's always tennis," I said.

Amy touched me on the cheek, laughing. "That's what I married you for, dear—that lovely ironic wit."

I hadn't known I was being witty, but I was willing to take full marks for anything.

"No, I know you wish the girls would try harder on the court," she said, "but you know perfectly well that all your tennis is really Leaf Out, that famous game you and your Valley Hunt Club friends used to play."

"Just what does that mean?"

"You'll have to work it out for yourself," she said, touching my lips with her index finger.

I bit it lightly and we let it go at that. But Leaf Out wasn't a bad way of getting on in the world—to fake the ritual, traditional game and vary it with personal rules, following the arbitrary accident to its end. Of course, the rules themselves had become almost too formalized in the last stages of our playing Leaf Out. Once David was gone the whole thing was over, except that, by that time, I had come to think of almost all of my life as a game of Leaf Out. I had come to accept that no matter how much I tried, no matter how many all-American conversations I mastered, I would never quite catch up, never quite find the means of translating my not quite American boyhood into the real thing. Because the real thing involved belief, and I could find no place for belief in this parody world.

I dozed after this—mercifully for everyone—because Junebug was knocking on the door and saying that supper would be ready soon. I must get up and prepare for another given scene, but this one at least I could view through the solvent of Old Rarity.

The next morning after breakfast George Kneller handled his four-wheel-drive Jeep competently but without real panache, following a faint track crossing the sloping land. We had driven well out of sight of the house and had said little for some time. At breakfast, just to keep things going, I had said something about feeling that Dalton lay in the heartland of the country.

George had taken me up by answering, "Right here we're in our own basin, you know. Most of us think *it's* the real center."

I murmured something about that being an interesting view.

He came back to this now, gesturing widely with his left hand and arm. "You can see how we keep it all together here. The Divide itself splits around us, so you don't have that feeling in the rest of the country of sliding off into one ocean or another."

"It's certainly self-containing," I said, "but that may be what you want."

"That's so," he said, shifting down to tackle the grade ahead.

"I probably felt like that in Dalton. I was just a small boy, and the only ocean I saw was a stationary one of cornfield after cornfield. 'Knee high by the Fourth of July!' they used to say. I don't suppose I thought of it then, but later I felt that you could easily drown in that particular ocean."

George Kneller stopped the Jeep at the top of the rise without responding to my remark. "This is about the best place to see it all. We'll get out and walk a short piece."

Before we'd left the house, he had lent me a red-and-green plaid mackinaw, a bit short in the sleeves, insisting I would be more comfortable in it than in my topcoat. He was right, I thought, as we walked a little distance down the slope from where he had parked the Jeep.

George stopped. "If you start at that little draw down there," he said, "and run a line due north to that small clump of brush by that outcrop, then west along the second low ridge, south to about an equal point in line with the little draw, you've pretty much got the Lloyd holding." He had moved his right arm about briskly, pointing, and I thought how typical it was that he would expect me to know due north and to pick up the outcrop immediately. All I cared about was seeing the land itself, so I nodded and scanned everything in sight.

"As you can see, it's all enclosed by my own land," he said. After a pause he went on, "I'd already been able to pick up the rest of that original holding."

"So if my Grandfather Lloyd had wanted to make use of his land you'd have had to grant him a right of way," I said. When I started the sentence I thought it would be a question, but it came out a flat statement.

He put a hand on my arm. "Yes, Tom, that's something that has been on my mind all these years, but what would any of you want to do that for?"

"Oh, I don't know," I said. "It would make a nice second place in the West for somebody. One of my cousins might like to play the gentleman rancher, you know, run a few head of cattle for the hell of it or the tax write-off—fly in to Latham every now and then."

His hand stayed on my arm. The thought of old Rob or, for that matter, myself, doing anything like that was too much. "I was just putting you on, George," I said. "I don't think any of us is the type. It must be obvious to you that I don't know zip about ranching."

"I'd begun to wonder," he said, his hand falling away.

"You know, the real reason the heirs have held on so long is that they can't bring themselves to believe that my Grandfather Lloyd picked up this land for nothing, for no special reason."

He wheeled on me. "But, Tom, that's exactly what happened. Your grandfather did pick up this land for nothing, or even less than nothing."

"I don't follow you."

"How else could he have got hold of it? He never saw it, he never had a notion of what it could be good for."

"Then I don't see why he bought it," I said, feeling just the least stir of family concern myself for Grandfather Lloyd's reputation.

"He didn't buy it. He picked it up because my half-brother, Rodney, was a fool about money—and a lot of other things, the poor dog."

"Your half-brother? I'm sorry, George, but I'm completely at sea."

"You mean you don't know how this property became part of your grandfather's estate?"

"I guess not."

"He owned it because Rod was back there in the north of Iowa with one of his hare-brained easy money schemes. He talked your grandfather into giving him a cash loan with this piece of land—the last of his assets—as security. No telling what he told your grandfather. Perhaps that's where all those wild ideas about minerals came in."

"Could be," I said automatically, trying to take in this revelation.

"Your grandfather must have been something of a soft touch, Tom. Not that old Rod wasn't a smooth enough talker, once he got started. But any shrewd banker would have seen through him like clear ice on a rain barrel. When the money scheme failed, Rod skipped and your grandfather was left holding the paper. I can say he handled all that well, sewed it up completely. But that's why I say he held it for nothing—he held it for a big fat goose egg in his books."

This struck George Kneller as funny and he chuckled.

I found it irritating to have him laughing at the expense of Grandfather Lloyd. He made this more acute by insisting, "Your grandfather must really have been a soft touch, Tom."

"Oh, I don't know," I heard myself saying. "True, the bank had to close, but in the end everyone got back a hundred cents on the dollar." I didn't say that it had crippled the family to manage this.

He relented a little. "Believe me, Tom, it was no disgrace for a small private bank to fail right after the First World War. I wasn't much more than married then, but banks were going down like rubber ducks. Most of them never got set up again."

Again he had entertained himself greatly. When he stopped laughing he said, "Why didn't anyone tell you about this, Tom?"

"Who knows?" I countered.

"Anyway, now you know."

"Now I know."

"Let's get back in the Jeep and I'll show you around some more."

After we had started rolling I asked, "Whatever became of Rodney?"

"What?"

"Your half-brother, Rod. What became of him?"

He hesitated. "He died not too long after all that."

"And it was you who had already bought out the better part of his land." Again I had started a question that ended as a statement.

He concentrated on his driving. Then he pointed at the hills to what I guessed was the north and said, "If you follow the horizon line there you'll see a small notch."

I spotted it. "Yes?"

"That's where we drive through to summer pasture," he said.

He turned the Jeep in a tight circle, picking up the track we had come by. We rode in silence for a time. Finally I said, "Thanks for bringing me out. At least one of my grandfather's descendants has looked at his land."

"Would you say that you find it good?" he surprised me by asking.

"The perfect question for a minister's son," I said, smiling. "I suppose I find it good, but I'm not too sorry to have it all settled. I've had to contend with Grandfather Lloyd all my life and this makes that a bit easier."

He jerked his head towards me. "But he's been dead for years."

"And hasn't Rodney been dead for years?"

"Rod?"

"Don't you ever think of what your grandchildren will think about you, and about your half-brother?"

"Never," he said, too quickly.

"You will, then, from now on," I said. "That's a fair enough trade. You get the rest of old Rod's property and everything that goes with it, past, present, and future. And as to being a grandfather, I notice that Junebug and Gladys didn't give you a George III."

We could see the house.

"You're quite a talker," he said.

"That's part of being both a Lloyd and a Jerome," I said. "In spite of everything, haven't you really been thinking about Rod most of the time?"

He pulled the Jeep up in front of the house. "Let's go in," he said. "You know, we're having quite a little get-together. Perhaps you'd like to freshen up."

In my room I changed into a checked brown flannel shirt, feeling sure my tweed jacket wouldn't quite do.

Junebug was waiting when I came out. His sweater reassured me. "There you are, Tom," he said. "I think everyone's in the old man's office, so I thought you might want to bring the papers with you."

I went back and picked up my briefcase.

George's office was jammed. Junebug's younger brother was there with his wife, and the Knellers' daughter with her husband. And the children. I didn't even try to sort them out.

George came over with my Old Rarity. "I want you to meet Jack Kroll, who's come by to help us." He led me over to a paunchy middle-aged man.

After we'd shaken hands, Kroll said, "You know, I'm sorry I can't stay, George, but I have to get on back to Latham, so if Mr. Jerome has his papers and power-of-attorney, we can do everything in two shakes of a lamb's tail."

I opened my briefcase and spread the papers out on the desk. Mr. Kroll took a perfunctory look at them. I signed my name three times, George Kneller signed his, and Kroll used his notary's seal. A mild cheer rose at the end of this.

Gladys came over and said, "You know this means a lot to Father."

"I'm sure," I said. "And it would have meant a good bit to his half-brother, Rodney, I dare say. By the way, was Rodney a Kneller?"

"What a strange thing to ask! How did you hear of him?"

"It was really *his* land, wasn't it?"

"I don't know much about that, but Rod wasn't a Kneller. He was a McMinn. His father died when he was quite young and then his mother married Greg Kneller. That was a long time ago."

"Did you know him at all?"

She fought away from this, saying, "I think it's time for us to eat. Just carry your glass along. You know, we weren't sure if a minister's son would drink."

"Who would have better cause?" I asked, and got no answer as we began trooping into the dining room, where the doors to the living room had been folded back. And there I saw a regular old-time Dalton buffet spread out. The children were helped first and the smaller ones seated at a table. The rest of us ate standing.

The Knellers and their in-laws came up to me in twos and threes. Their very politeness made me feel more and more a foreigner here.

In a slack moment I slipped away, went to my room and packed my things. I got my bag out through the front door and into the Chevy without anyone seeing me.

Back at the party, I went up to Grace Kneller and said, "I hope you won't feel I'm being rude, but there's still a good bit of driving time left today and I'm sure everyone will be glad to have the papers processed as soon as possible. You've all been very kind."

She called over to her husband, "George, Tom Jerome thinks he must leave us. Why, there's no hurry in the world, and you fit in so well, Tom. Why, the very idea!"

George came over protesting, "Spend at least another day with us, Tom."

"Thanks, but you know I still have a long way to go."

I wasn't sure how sincere the chorus of protests sounded, but almost all the adults followed me out to the car.

"It's been great to be here," I said, "and to see Rodney McMinn's Wyoming acreage. I'll remember this visit the rest of my life, and I'm sure you'll all remember me when you mine the uranium."

That really stopped them cold. Then George Kneller let out a shout of laughter. "You're just as crazy as if you were all Lloyd, Tom!"

I started up the motor, raced it, and hoped it wouldn't stall in the cold. The Chevy came on bravely and I waved as I moved off.

Not, I thought, a bad exit.

8 🙊

I HAD SCOUTED out the land. I had represented my tribe and even got hold of a small handle on the otherwise complacently landlocked Knellers—Rodney McMinn, black sheep, smooth talker. Whatever secrets about Rod they held in their hearts behind those antlered sweaters I might never know. That brief, understated contest out by the Wyoming acreage with George Kneller remained unresolved. It made me think of the struggle that had gone on in Dalton between my Lloyd cousins and Bert Kratz for the leadership of the boys and their club.

Now I wanted to get to Dalton both in the flesh and in memory. I felt guiltily un-American about my memories. I knew that the Fourth of July and going to the Barnum and Bailey, Ringling Brothers Circus in Center City ought to be the two great events of that summer. I remembered them well enough, one with its speeches and fireworks and baseball game—Uncle Drew calling the balls and strikes—the other with the first *tableaux vivants* I'd seen and the disturbingly curved, bulging, pink-clad bodies of the trapeze artists.

But what struck me as important now was the way my confusions had kept getting me deeper and deeper into trouble. I couldn't even be sure of arranging them in the correct order, because some of my sins weighed more heavily than others. I ranked them as my sin of pride, then putting myself into Mrs. Hauser's work-reddened hands, then Mr. Carter's plug nickel, and above all my final, my unforgivable sin—my betrayal of the boys to the girls.

I couldn't say that Rob and Brooks weren't honest when they suggested that I might want to join their club, made up of almost all the Dalton boys between the ages of ten and fifteen. I was young for this, but I had, as they knew, one superlative qualification for membership—an allowance of fifty cents a week.

The club's single activity, if it could be called that, was its attempt to finish building the clubhouse—a ramshackle affair of packing boxes and tar paper on a vacant lot across from Uncle Drew and Aunt Harriet's place. When not working at this, the members herded together if they had no chores and went swimming in a water hole full of mudsuckers a mile down the railroad tracks under a culvert, or just sat around in the heat, rolling cigarettes of corn silk and choking over them.

I didn't mind when Brooks and Rob said I could buy my way in. The money that Mr. Carter and Grandma Tessy had given me would come in handy. At least I had sense enough to say nothing about my hoard. What the club really needed, they said, and Bert Kratz agreed, was some ready cash for nails. The propped up sides of the clubhouse could be made more solid, and they thought they could pick up an old door somewhere.

"How much would it cost for me to belong?" I asked.

"That depends on . . . " Bert Kratz began. Brooks interrupted, "If you could give your allowance for one week that would get you in. Then we figure a nickel a week keeps everyone a member, but plenty of times someone has to skip his dues for a while, especially these days."

"Is that what everyone pays to get in?" I knew right away that wasn't a good question.

Bert Kratz said, "You aren't as old as most of us. Neither is Phil." He had turned away from me and I saw he was looking at someone coming towards us. It was the red-haired boy I'd seen in church.

We sat in the dust beside the clubhouse and he joined us. "Hi, Phil," Brooks said.

Bert said, "Listen, Phil, don't you owe the club some money?"

"No, I don't," Phil said. "You're a rotten treasurer, Bert. I told you you'd probably forget to enter it in the club accounts."

"Don't give me that," Bert said, jumping up.

"Then don't try twisting my arm," Phil said.

"Who's going to stop me?"

"Come on, Bert," Rob said quietly. "Why pick on someone smaller than you and in the club? Maybe you did forget."

"Let's skip it for now," Brooks said. "Anyway, Tom, this is Phil Creighton. Mr. Creighton is—was—the teller in the bank. Phil, this is our Chinese cousin, Tom Jerome. He's going to join the club."

Phil said "Hello" to me and I said "Hello" to him. The older boys began arguing about something and Phil moved across and settled down by me. "I saw you in church a while back," he said.

"I saw you too."

Then Brooks called over to us. "Tom, the club is pretty well broke. We haven't been able to buy any nails for two or three weeks."

"I could get my initiation fee now and bring it back," I said.

"That's a good idea," Bert Kratz said.

"And be sure to enter it in the account book if you've really got one," Phil said.

Bert made a move to get up again, half-threatening, but Phil thumbed his nose at him, something I wouldn't have had the nerve to do.

"It's kind of late to do much today," Bert said and the others agreed. The meeting broke up, so only Brooks, Rob, Bert Kratz, and Phil came along with me to the house.

Brooks said, "Why don't we let Tom get his money and meet us down by the barn?"

No one in the house noticed me as I went up to our room and got fifty cents out of my rolled up stockings. Back by the barn, I gave the money to Bert, who said, "I expect Pop wants me back at the store. Tomorrow we'll get some nails and get back to work on the clubhouse."

I thought I should be admitted to the club in some formal way, thinking about the Round Table and being dubbed a knight or at least getting rank as a squire. All that happened, though, was that Phil said, "Gee, Tom, I'm glad you're in the club. You must be the youngest now, but still about my age. You know, with the bank closing it's really something."

"We'll manage," Brooks said. I didn't know what he meant. I wondered if Phil's father was completely out of a job. Uncle Drew and Uncle Fred still went to the bank to do something called "working on the books."

"Bert's a lazy, fat-bottomed bugger," Brooks said.

"And a bully," Phil said.

"You shouldn't lay yourself open," Rob said.

"I know." Phil pushed a hand through his red hair. "Sometimes I just can't help it."

"Right," Brooks said, "but you should try."

"Why don't we pitch a few games of horseshoes before we all go home?" Rob suggested. "We've been trying to teach Tom. He wants to use that tricky over-and-over throw." All four of us headed for the barn.

"It looks good," Phil said, turning to me, "but it's risky."

"I know," I said, "but I don't seem to get the hang of the other way. I'm really not very good at any game except tennis."

"Wow!" Phil exclaimed.

"You really play tennis, Tom?" Brooks asked.

"Sure," I said. "I usually get somewhere near the finals in the under-twelve summer tournaments."

"There's no place to play tennis around here or even in Center City, I guess," Rob said. "I don't know that I'd say anything about playing tennis around the club, Tom."

"Oh?"

"Yeah," Brooks said. "Rob's right. There's nothing wrong with tennis. It's a real classy game—Big Bill Tilden and all that. But in Dalton tennis may be just a bit *too* classy. People might get the wrong idea."

"It's about the only game Father thinks I can be good at," I said. "I won't mention it if you say not to."

"Dad played tennis in college," Rob said. "He won some kind of tournament."

"I'll say," Brooks said. "He played so well he flunked out his freshman year."

Rob looked angry. "You know we aren't supposed to mention that."

"No, and there's a lot of other things we can't mention either," Brooks said.

"Let's break it up," Rob said. He turned to Phil. "How about you and me taking on Brooks and Tom?"

"It seems to me Tom and I would make a good team," Phil said. "We're about the same age."

"We'd beat your asses off," Brooks said.

"Maybe so, maybe not," Phil said. "How about it, Tom?"

"Anyone who has me for a partner is going to lose, at least in the beginning," I said. "If *you* don't mind, it's fine with me."

"You shouldn't talk that way," Phil said. "And who knows, anyway?"

"Come on then and be slaughtered," Brooks said, grinning.

Phil and Brooks walked to the farther stake. Rob said to me in a low voice, "Phil's good, and he can get under a guy's skin and rattle him. Still, I don't think you've much hope."

"I don't want you to *try* to lose," I said.

"Don't worry. It would be harder for me to try to lose than to win. Phil and Brooks would know right off."

"Let's get on with it," Brooks called. "What are you guys having—a committee meeting? After all, you're enemies."

"I was just reminding Tom of the fundamentals," Rob said.

"Fundamentals!" Phil called back. "What do you buzzards think we are, just a couple of beginners?"

"Tom sure as heck is," Brooks said.

"Maybe," Phil said. "But you can tell a lot about how somebody can pitch from the way he walks and picks up a shoe."

"You're in for a big fat surprise, buddy," Brooks insisted. "Go ahead, and I'll knock off any leaner or come down on any ringer if you're that lucky."

"No you don't! We'll flip for the start."

"With what?" Brooks asked. "We're all broke."

"I've got a few pennies in my pocket," I said.

"The family millionaire!" Brooks said. "I thought missionaries were all poor."

We had met between the stakes, so I didn't need to say that though I was poorer than my business classmates in Shanghai they had no real standing, what with their fathers being in trade.

"I'll toss," Rob said, taking a penny from me, "and Phil can call it."

As the penny turned in the air, Phil sang out, "Heads heads under the beds!" And heads—an Indian head—it miraculously was.

"I knew it!" Phil said. "We may be the kids, but we've got the brains."

I wondered what he would have said for tails.

"I'll go second," Phil said, and I could see that Brooks was a little irritated.

Brooks came close to a ringer with his first shoe, but it circled and flipped off away from the stake. "Boy, is that going to be hard to beat!" Phil said, throwing short, just hitting the edge of the pocket. His shoe skidded up against the stake.

Brooks' second shoe came down nicely. As it settled it clanked against Phil's. Instead of ringing, it kicked up into a leaner. "Oho!" Phil crowed. He sent his second shoe spinning straight in, fast and flat, knocking the leaner away and leaving his first shoe right there against the stake.

Brooks sounded a bit strained as he said, "Great pitch!"

"It was just luck," Phil said. "I know as well as you do that you're a lot better most of the time than I am." The way he said it made it sound too polite, and Brooks made a face.

"What did I tell you?" Rob whispered.

"Well, you won't have any trouble with me," I said, meaning it.

"Don't *you* try the same game on *me,* Tom. It's up to you to start because you're ahead."

I let go with my over-and-over delivery. At least I didn't overshoot the stake as my shoe jumped a bit and skidded forward.

"Nothing to advertise in the Police Gazette," Rob said, "but respectable." I felt better.

Rob wasn't as graceful as Brooks, who ended his pitch with a waving gesture, his left arm out and his feet closing like a ballet dancer's, but Rob delivered a businesslike pitch and his shoe settled down a ringer. Brooks clapped and Phil said, "I always thought Rob was better than you, Brooks. Now give it a real smashing whirl, Tom."

I did get my shoe up in a nice arc and as it hit it clanked against Rob's, bouncing off without dislodging it. Rob's second pitch came down close, not quite on target, kicking into my shoe and pushing it closer.

And that was about the way it went. Phil could get into Brooks often enough to keep things interesting, but I hadn't a chance against Rob, who obviously wasn't going to ease up.

We were into our third game, which was a lot closer than anything Brooks had expected, I knew, when Rob said in a low voice to me, "Well, well, well, I do believe we have someone taking a gander at us. Don't give yourself away, Tom, but when you can, take a look under the locust trees by the barn."

That was where Uncle Drew and Uncle Fred had stood that first Sunday afternoon. I supposed they were there again with their flat brown bottle of moonshine. But when I got a chance to look over that way I saw Bert Kratz leaning against the farthest tree.

When my next turn came and he saw my style, he laughed loud enough for us to hear and came out of the shadows. "What the hell kind of way is that for a beginner to pitch?" he asked.

"I'm from China," I heard myself saying firmly, "and even if nobody stoops to pitching horseshoes there, I think they would pitch the way I'm trying to."

I knew I was partly imitating Phil saying this, and Bert's movement forward was like his threatening step earlier at the club meeting. But then with my second pitch I got my first solid ringer of the match.

"Not bad," Bert said grudgingly.

"Thank you very much," I said automatically. He glared at me without speaking, but strolled towards us.

"Listen, Bert," I said, "if you'd like to pitch a game you could take my place. You know I'm just learning, and even if I do use that showoff way I bet I could pick up some pointers from you."

I hadn't meant anything in particular. It was just the way I'd been brought up in the mission. If there's an extra person around you ought to do something about bringing him into the circle. Thinking of this now, I couldn't tell if everyone actually stood still for a long time or if I'd lengthened the pause in my memory. But at least all five of us were caught motionless for a space.

Bert broke it up by taking a couple of steps forward. "Well, say . . . " he began and stopped. Then he shrugged and said, "It's late, and I think I'd better be getting back to Pop at the store." Since that was what he had said earlier it didn't make sense to me.

"I'd better be getting on home myself," Phil said. We all shifted. Phil came over to me as Bert started around the far side of the house. Brooks and Rob headed for the barn with the horseshoes.

When he reached me, Phil said, "That was a good try, Tom."

I thought he meant the way I'd played. "I'll keep at it," I said. "If I'd been better we might have taken one of those games."

"Oh, that," Phil said. "Brooks is fun to tease. I don't think he minds as much as he lets on. But I meant about asking Bert in."

"Oh?"

"Yeah," he said, "it was a good idea, but it's probably too late. Still, you can't tell."

"Anyway," I said, "thanks for being my partner."

I don't know how long it took me to understand that what Phil had been talking about when he said it was too late to ask Bert in hadn't anything to do with the time of day. It may not have hit me, so far as that goes, until after the summer at Dalton had ended. But I could certainly see now how late it had been if no one had asked Bert in before.

It must have been around this time, maybe on a Sunday, that Fran asked Mother about something that had puzzled her that first time in church and that I had completely forgotten. But at least it was by the time I'd grown familiar enough with the disorderly services to ignore them completely and play my own games.

"It was something about riding in front of the rain," Fran said.

"I'm surprised anyone remembers," Mother said, smiling. "Probably it's just because there are some things that become important to the person they happen to and to everyone else as well."

She looked straight ahead as she said this, the way she had done more than once since we'd arrived in Dalton. Fran and I waited, because we'd learned that Mother had been thrown back into the past when she did this, and once she came out of it she almost always said something surprising, something that didn't quite fit into our standard mission family life.

"I was out riding," she began, almost dreamily. "You know what I mean, *riding*—not *driving* in a motor car, but *riding*. I was back from the university in Madison one summer and sometimes I saddled up Papa's frisky mare, Morgana, in the afternoon and rode out along the section roads and trails—just to get away for a while."

I wanted to ask away from what, but Fran got in ahead of me as she said, "What a pretty name!"

Mother was still smiling and looking into the distance. "Isn't it?" she said. "Papa called her that because she was at least three-quarters Morgan."

"Morgan le Fay was one of King Arthur's sisters, wasn't she?" I asked.

"Everyone knows that," Fran said, "and you shouldn't interrupt. Let Mother go on."

I wanted to say that *she* was the one who had interrupted, after all, but Mother was already back in the past. "That afternoon," she said, "I'd just ridden off without any special place to go. Morgana hadn't been out much lately and was both naturally frisky, which made me pay attention to her, and fat, which made her want to stop suddenly. All I did was keep her going. It's hard to explain, but coming back to Dalton that summer from Madison was in many ways one of the longest trips I'd taken. I suppose I was thinking about that and rode much farther than usual. I didn't really pay attention until Morgana began tossing her head and snorting, sidling impatiently. I started to straighten her when I looked ahead and saw that a storm was coming in from the west. There I was on Morgana, and I hadn't bothered to change into my regular habit and use the sidesaddle. I'd just slung on Papa's English saddle and put on a pair of work pants I'd found in the tack room."

"How exciting!" Fran said, interrupting again. I knew better than to point this out to her.

"Yes," Mother said, "it was. I didn't want to get caught in the storm, so I wheeled Morgana around and made a bee-line for Dalton and the barn. Morgana wasn't much of a jumper, and there weren't all that many ditches, so most of the time I could follow the dirt roads. I wanted to beat the storm not only because I knew they might worry about my being out in it but also because I thought of what I would look like coming in wet and dressed in some hired man's pants riding astride."

Fran nodded, though this didn't make much sense to me.

"At first I could *see* the storm coming if I looked around, and then I could *hear* it getting closer, and finally I could *smell* it coming on behind me. I kicked Morgana into a gallop and lashed her a couple of times across her withers with the loose reins we used then, and there we were pelting across fields, taking ditches and every now and then a low gate. It had been a dry season, so we raised lots of dust and my plan for getting back without calling attention turned around on me. I used to think afterwards that everyone in town and for two miles to the west had seen Emma Lloyd riding astride hell for leather—excuse me!—for the Lloyd barn."

"Did you make it?" Fran asked. I thought to myself that I'd never before heard Mother so carried away by anything.

"Just barely," Mother said, her head back and her eyes shining. "I came up that last stretch behind the barn and I knew I'd wind Morgana if I held her at that pace much longer; so I reined her in just enough to let *her* get caught by a few drops, and then I gave her her head and she came the last few furlongs on her own, the storm just brushing us as we galloped in before it. What a ride that was!"

"It sounds wonderful," Fran said.

"It was," Mother said. "Afterwards, though, when I'd skinned out of the pants, put on my own clothes, rubbed down Morgana and thrown a blanket over her, and the storm had passed, you'd have thought the whole world had been watching. The next day people dropped by the bank, asking Papa if I was all right and could it be true I wasn't riding sidesaddle. It turned into a little bit of local history, I suppose."

"I'm glad you told us," Fran said.

"Me, too," I put in, "even if it was a funny thing to put into a sermon."

In spite of all the food and drink I'd had at the Knellers' I found myself growing hungry. At the next town I hit I pulled up by a diner and went in for coffee and doughnuts. I took my map with me, and as I let my second cup of coffee cool I saw that I must soon begin angling up to the northeast. Whether I would really save time I wasn't sure, but at least on paper it looked as if some of the secondary roads would cut off quite a few miles. I reflected for a moment or two on Father's disapproval of this sort of adventuring, going beyond the safe bounds of the Auto Club's authority.

Back in the Chevy and on the lookout for the particular road I'd settled on, I wondered how long I had known that summer that another nickel's worth of nails or brads or whatever would make no difference in finishing the clubhouse, that its actual importance lay in its never being finished so that we could tinker with it and meet by it and talk about how great it would be when it finally got done, though no one said what it would be great for.

I kept thinking of my plug nickel. I'd inspected it lots of times alone in my alcove. It looked like every other nickel I'd seen and sounded like every other nickel I'd rung by this time—not that nickels really rang. Fran and I knew a good bit about coins from the silver currency in Shanghai, with the exchange rate changing by the hour, and I couldn't help thinking that my plug nickel was an amazingly good piece of counterfeiting.

The pressure built in me. I felt disloyal in not letting the club know that I had this piece of money. Finally, one Saturday afternoon when Brooks and Rob, Phil and I sat outside the clubhouse—that being several degrees cooler than the inside—I said, "I don't know if it's any help or not, but when we were leaving Shanghai, a man in the mission gave me some American money. I've given all of it to the club now except for a plug nickel. Do you suppose a plug nickel would be worth anything at all?"

"Gee, I've never seen a plug nickel," Phil said. "What's it look like?"

"Just a regular nickel as far as I can see."

"You have it with you?" Rob asked.

"No, but I can get it," I said.

I ran to the house. As I went upstairs I heard Grandma Tessy moving about in her room. I hoped she wouldn't call out for anything. Our room stood empty, so I dug the nickel out of the black stockings, slipped it into my right hip pocket, and scooted down the stairs and out the front door without anyone's seeing me. I felt both guilty and relieved, thinking that at last someone else would know about it and I wouldn't be alone in having to decide what to do with it.

Brooks reached for the coin and put on one of his performances, holding the nickel at arm's length. "Aha!" he said. "So this is a *gen-you-wine* plug nickel, is it?"

"That's what the Reverend Mr. Carter told me," I said, "and he's an ordained Presbyterian minister. He said it could be a good luck piece, but how can bad money bring good luck?"

Phil took the nickel from Brooks. "It feels all right to me."

"I can't see anything wrong with it," Brooks said. "Why don't we take it down to Kratz's and buy as much stuff as we can for it?"

"It's really Tom's," Rob said, "so you shouldn't decide."

"Would we be arrested if we got caught?" I asked.

Brooks laughed. "Arrested for five fake cents in Dalton? I think not, my boy."

"I don't know," I said, feeling responsible for everyone's moral fate. "I just don't know—you can see it looks like a good nickel, but since it's really a plug—well, I don't know."

"I've got an idea," Phil said. "If you let one of *us* have it—if you *gave* it to one of us, you'd give it away and then *we* can spend it."

"That's a terrific idea," Brooks said.

"It's up to Tom," Rob insisted.

"I don't know," I said again, wishing that I'd not only never mentioned the plug nickel, but also that Mr. Carter had never given it to me.

Brooks was the oldest, so finally I said, "You want it, Brooks?"

"Sure thing," he said, reaching for the nickel. "I'm taking it and thank you very much, my generous Chinese cousin." He bowed to me as he went on, "Let's go right down to old man Kratz's and spend it."

"I hope Bert isn't there," I said.

"What would it matter?" Phil asked.

"I'm not sure—I just know I hope he isn't there."

We walked the three blocks to Main Street, Brooks tossing the nickel every few steps, watching it turn over and settle into his palm.

In Kratz's a farmer and his wife stood looking over some dry goods. I couldn't see Bert anywhere and I felt a little better.

Then Brooks, instead of going into the hardware section, stopped at the candy counter right next to the cash register. "Look," he said, "the nails we can buy with this won't help the clubhouse very much, will they?"

"I guess we all know that," Rob said.

"So why not just enjoy ourselves?" Brooks asked.

Before anyone said anything Mr. Kratz moved his bulk towards us slowly. "Well, young gentlemen," he said, "how can I be of service to you?"

"I've got a nickel here," Brooks said, "and I wondered how many pieces of hard candy it would buy."

"Let's see," Mr. Kratz said. "Since there's four of you I could let you have, say, five pieces each, and five separate flavors."

Twenty pieces of candy struck me as a real bargain, but I knew we shouldn't be buying it. Not only was there the risk of being caught passing counterfeit money; we weren't even spending it for the common good but for our own sinful self-indulgence.

My remorse came too late. I'd given the nickel away and Mr. Kratz had already dropped it into the register. He put our candy into a small brown paper bag and handed it to Brooks.

"That's swell, Mr. Kratz, and thank you very much," Brooks said, passing the bag around right there in front of the counter. I took a piece and felt very daring for a couple of minutes as we walked out and went back up the street toward the clubhouse. The others were laughing and saying how easy it had been and what a great idea it had been to get candy instead of nails.

I tried to think they were right, that we hadn't cheated anyone, but I knew I was fooling myself. We sat down on the shady side of the clubhouse, which would never be finished now. The candy lasted a long time in my mouth. I knew from something I'd read that it ought to make me sick or at least taste like ashes, but it didn't. I ate my full share and enjoyed the blending of peppermint with winter-green, cherry with lime, and finally the over-sweet, artificial strength of grape.

Not until we'd broken up to go home for supper did the full wickedness of what we'd done hit me. I went around back of the barn and tried to throw up. It didn't work. It just brought all the blended flavors back into my mouth and they still tasted good. I went in through the kitchen door feeling worse than ever.

9 🕊

I'M NOT SURE just when Fran and I began to see that Aunt Louise, though she wasn't exactly unfriendly, didn't approve of something about us. We couldn't understand this because both of us had begun to do things that we'd never done in Shanghai. Not only did we make our own beds in the morning, but if either of us was around when anyone in the kitchen needed more corncobs for the stove we lugged them in from the great pile in the barn in a bushel basket. I thought this might give me a little edge on Fran for once and I confronted her with it.

"You used to keep telling me about how everything was in America because you remembered it all and I was too young to remember anything," I said, "but you never said anything about the kind of work around the house our relatives do. I suppose it's because the bank is busted and they're saving money."

I should have known better, I realized, as soon as she said, "Don't be ridiculous. After all, I was just four-and-a-half when we went back, and it's remarkable that I remember everything so well. But you wouldn't expect anyone that age to do chores."

"I guess not," I said, hoping she wouldn't be angry.

"And anyway, Tom," she went on, "we didn't spend much time out here in the sticks. We were living on Riverside Drive in New York most of the time. That's quite a different world."

I wasn't sure what "in the sticks" meant and didn't want to ask, so I said, "I've overheard Aunt Louise talking to Mother a couple of times when they didn't know I could hear her . . ."

"Tom, you know with that's called—eavesdropping—and it isn't something a proper person does."

"I didn't *mean* to hear her," I said.

"What did she say?"

"Are you sure you want to hear what I overheard?"

"Don't tease me, Tom. I suppose it was something about the way we've been brought up in China."

I tried not to sound deflated. "In a way, I guess. But she was saying something about our living in America—not China—and how we might be at a loss later on. How could we be at a loss?"

Fran shrugged. "I don't know exactly, but you can see what Aunt Louise expects from Martha."

What Aunt Louise expected from us became clear one morning when she had come over a little after breakfast and we were all still in the kitchen.

"Emma," she said, speaking to Mother, "don't you think Fran and Tom might at least look after what walnuts there are out front? They're starting to fall, and they could pick them up and hull them and put them out to dry."

Mother looked worried, and I thought it must be because Aunt Louise had said "at least," because that had made me angry.

"Those two old trees don't bear as well as they used to, but there's no point in letting the crop go to waste, especially nowadays," Aunt Louise said. "At the moment, the walk is quite untidy."

"Would you mind, children?" Mother asked, looking at us, and I could see Aunt Louise stiffen.

"We wouldn't mind a bit," Fran said, and I knew she was answering Aunt Louise more than she was Mother.

And we didn't mind very much at first. We got a couple of bushel baskets from the barn and gathered the fallen nuts. The next day Uncle Drew came over and shook the trees with a long pole. After we'd gathered up everything that fell, and cleared the lawn as well as the walk, we faced the problem of hulling the nuts. A few had already split and we could rip the hulls off, but most of the hulls were still hard.

At first we treated them gently, having been told often enough of the superiority of native American black walnuts over the blander English ones we got in Shanghai. "Insipid!" Mother used to say of those. "Just wait till you get home and taste some real walnuts."

We knew we should feel privileged to handle this rare food. We made no headway until we found we could split the hulls by throwing the nuts down hard on the cement walk between the street and the front porch. Even then, it was strenuous work, and we might have to smash one down two or three times. But we kept at it, knowing we mustn't let Mother down as we split hull after hull on the walk, then ripped off the green juicy covering and tossed it into a basket before we put the nut on an old sheet spread out in the sunlight for drying.

After spending the better part of an afternoon at this, we had gone inside to see if we could get a snack in the kitchen, when Aunt Louise walked over to the house from her apartment. We heard her in the front hall, asking loudly in what even then I thought was a sort of theatrical voice, "Who has *ruined* the front walk?"

That sounded so funny to me that I laughed as we came out of the kitchen, followed by Mother, who said, "What in the world are you shouting about Louise?"

"I am not *shouting!*" Aunt Louise declared. "I am just *asking* about the *ruination* of the front walk. It is streaked black, absolutely *black* with walnut stains!"

"Oh dear!" Mother said. "What has happened, children?"

"We've been cracking the hulls on the walk," Fran said. "It was the only way we could find to split them."

"Oh dear!" Mother said again.

"Just think of how it will *look* to everyone!" Aunt Louise said. "Never, *never,* has that walk been anything but *clean,* and now, *now,* what will the town think, especially *now,* with everyone watching us, to have the walk, the *white* cement walk to the *Lloyd* house, *filthy* with walnut stains?"

Grandma Tessy appeared at the top of the stairs, wrapped in a flowered peignoir, her thinning hair pinned back. "Whatever is

going on?" she asked, looking frightened. "What has happened
now?"

"Fran and Tom have *blackened* the front walk with *walnut* juice,"
Aunt Louise called up to her. "It's a disgraceful mess!'

"Now, Louise . . . " Mother began.

"Anyway, that is what *I* feel," Aunt Louise said, a little less
certainly now. And whatever reason she had come for she must have
forgotten, because she walked out the front door without another
word.

Grandma Tessy and Mother looked at each other. Grandma Tessy
said, "I suppose something should be done. Louise is so touchy these
days. It's a shame, but then . . . "

"It's my fault," Mother said. "I just didn't think about it."

"Oh, fault, fault!" Grandma Tessy burst out. "Why must everything be someone's *fault?* It's the way life is, that's all—it's just the
way life is!" She began to cry.

"Now, Tessy," Mother said, "you must think of yourself and not
take on this way."

"I'm sorry," Grandma Tessy said, wiping her eyes. "It's just that
sometimes people are so *stern,* so sure they're *right,* that they *know.*
Well, it simply isn't true."

"No, of course not," Mother said.

Grandma Tessy stood there, leaning against the banister until she
said, "I must go back and rest."

Mother turned to us and said, "It was foolish to stain the walk, but
nobody told you about walnut juice. We'll see what we can
manage."

During the next couple of days we found very little to manage
with. We tried mopping with soap and water, then scrubbing with
soap and water, down on our hands and knees. We tried scouring
powder. Those stains resisted everything.

"What'll they do to us?" I asked Fran.

"They won't *do* anything," she said. "It's just what they'll *look,*
what they'll *think.*"

She was right. Everyone except Mother and Grandma Tessy

either avoided looking at us or assumed a sort of superior attitude when speaking. On Mrs. Hauser's next day for housework we saw her standing there by the walk for a while before coming around the house to the kitchen door. That was the final disgrace, to have Mrs. Hauser, Heidi's mother, laughing at us. I felt it strongly because I still held my feeling about the war and the Huns, and I thought of Hauser as a German name and I felt troubled by Heidi's relation to the other children in Dalton.

After Mrs. Hauser had gathered the laundry that noon she came to Fran and me as we crouched beside the walk, halfheartedly trying some new scouring powder on a long streak. "Now I tell you," Mrs. Hauser said, "I come back tomorrow. I fix it." She walked off without turning and before either of us could tell her it was hopeless.

We had no idea what she could mean, but next morning early she was on the front walk with a pail and a big scrub brush. We knew it was no use and I felt especially guilty, feeling as I did about the Hausers. Fran and I went out to tell her she should stop trying.

She looked up as we came beside her and said, "You see?" Sure enough, the walk was white where she had scrubbed.

"Why, we tried everything, Mrs. Hauser!" Fran said.

"Everything but strong lye," she said, dipping her red scarred hands into the bucket to wet the brush again.

"Lye!" Fran said. "You'll burn yourself, Mrs. Hauser."

"Takes more than lye to burn Old Lady Hauser," she said, grinning up at us, showing how many teeth she had lost. She brought out the brush and scrubbed away.

I knew I was witnessing a miracle.

"We were the ones who did it," Fran said. "You shouldn't have to do this, Mrs. Hauser. Perhaps if we got gloves . . . "

"I *do* do it," Mrs. Hauser said, not pausing in her scrubbing. "I do it because never has your grandfather turned me away. Even when I got a little drunk, when I have a baby, you know," she said, "he never say anything to make me feel bad. That is why I do this and I do it, too, because your mother is a good woman and because you play with Heidi."

That made me feel even worse, because though it was true that Heidi played with Fran and the other girls, she was always on the edge of things, and I wasn't the only one who spoke about her being a German, a Hun, a Boche.

"I don't know how we can ever thank you enough, Mrs. Hauser," Fran said.

"Thank you is not needed," Mrs. Hauser said. "No, thank you is not needed."

And there was the walk to the Lloyd house white again—possibly, we thought, whiter than it had been before, because Mrs. Hauser had scrubbed its entire length. I bore a double guilt now whenever Heidi was around, because I couldn't say I felt much more friendly than before, and I suspected Fran felt the same way.

But if I hadn't got out of that, I thought, jeering at myself and my academic need for a transition, I was almost out of Wyoming. As I rounded a turn I saw the North Platte below me in the fading light, and by the time I had reached and crossed it I knew that the pale rising glow ahead marked Scottsbluff, Nebraska, where I would stop. I had a good chance of reaching Dalton the next day, but I put off calling Martha.

Amy had told me to wait until I was in the old Lloyd house before I called home in California. "You mustn't worry about us," she'd said. "Just take your time and relax. You make too big a deal out of these things sometimes, not that it won't be great to have all that stuff from the past decently buried."

"I'm sure you're right," I'd said. "I suppose 'decently' is the operative word."

She answered with nothing more than a wry twitch of her lips. I followed my usual routine in Scottsbluff the next morning, gassing up early and buying a sandwich and an apple for lunch. Once on the road, I thought I might hit Sioux Falls early enough to know if I could reach Dalton by nightfall. Tuning the radio, I brought in an Omaha station with a weather report. A small snowstorm had fallen across the plains, not enough to block the roads, but only to make them tricky here and there. A strong new front was developing far in the north that might bring on something serious, but it was still too early to say.

Though I hadn't reached what I thought of as home country yet in relation to Dalton I had got into silo—"pagoda"—land. Remembering how alone I had felt when Mother and Fran had laughed at me over that, I thought of how alone I had felt that summer when everything seemed to conspire to betray me into Bert Kratz's trap. I'd grown so used to hanging around with the club members, never being in the center except when I had some money, but never being completely outside as long as Phil or Brooks or Rob was there that I'd almost forgotten all the pressures and rivalries. But when the whole plot opened, Phil and his folks had gone to Lakeview for a couple of weeks. Uncle Fred remarked to Uncle Drew, "Creighton must have had a little extra in a sock somewhere," and Uncle Drew said, "We're all scraping up odds and ends until we get the books settled. It can't be all that bad, you know. After all, Papa may have been extended . . . " and then he noticed me and in a different voice said, "Well there, Tom, and how is the great horseshoe pitcher today?"

"They don't laugh so much at me now," I said. "I'm really getting the hang of it."

"Good for you," he said, but I could tell he really wasn't interested.

Before the Creightons left, Phil had said if I could get someone to drive me over I should spend a couple of days with them, but this hadn't worked out because Brooks had picked up a weekday job on a farm out of town, and Uncle Fred had found something for Rob to do for a few days down at the grain elevator by the tracks.

When Bert said, "You know, we ought to work up a little excitement around here," he sounded innocent enough.

Rusty Blair, his particular crony, said, "Yeah, but what kind of excitement can you work up on hot days like this in a dead town like Dalton with the bank busted and all the rest?"

Bert took a quick look at me. "I was thinking it might be exciting to pull a trick on the girls," he said. "You know, they're always so snotty about everything. They laugh at the clubhouse. We ought to teach them a lesson."

I thought about Fran and Martha and the other girls, Heidi with them. They usually gathered outside someone's house or got called in to help with some kitchen job. I couldn't think that anything to do with them would be very exciting. I didn't really listen to Bert for a while as he kept talking. After all, he usually ignored me just as he did Phil unless he could find a special reason to pick on us.

Then I heard Bert say, "And I think the bugger who gets to lead them into the trap will be good little, rich little Tom."

I saw he was looking at me and I asked, "What kind of trap, and why *me?*"

"Haven't you been listening?"

"Maybe not very much," I said. "I'm not terribly interested in girls, you know."

Bert and Rusty and some of the older guys laughed. Rusty said, "Yeah, you're really skinny and pretty young still."

"I just don't think they do very exciting things," I said. That brought another laugh and I felt troubled, thinking that I'd a lot rather be doing something with Fran than listening to a stupid plan of Bert's.

Still, I had to listen to him now as he said, "I've got to admit you talk smoother than most of us. If you tell them somebody's hurt bad in the barn you can make them believe it."

"Maybe it should be Tom who's hurt," someone said. "That would be sure to bring them in."

"That's what I call real dumb," Bert said. "If it's Tom who's hurt, how can he go and get them to come into the barn to help?"

By now I wished I'd been listening all along. "How is anyone going to get hurt?" I asked. "And why would you run for the girls instead of a doctor?"

"No one's *really* getting hurt, kid," Bert said. "You get someone like Martha to listen and she'll come running to help."

"Then what?"

"We'll be up in the loft of the Lloyd barn," he said. "We'll have this rope strung out like a lasso at the bottom of the ladder, and when Martha—the first girl, I guess—steps into it we pull up the rope and capture her."

"What for?" I asked. Some of them snickered.

"We chase the rest of the girls out and hold her hostage."

"But why?"

"We could tease her, you know. Make her give us some kisses or something like that, just for the fun of it."

"It doesn't sound like much fun to me," I persisted.

"That shows how much *you* know, Chinky," Rusty said.

"I may not know a lot," I said, "but anyone who has to tie up a girl to make her do something can't be good for very much."

That did it. That was the last thing in the world I should have said with no one there to back me up. I thought I'd found my place in Dalton, especially with the boys. I acted the clown with my showoff horseshoe pitching and my international accent.

This was different, with Bert saying, "Anyway, that's what *you're* going to do, Tom. And if you mess up it's the end for you."

"The end?" I asked.

No one said anything. I guessed Bert meant I couldn't be in the club or something like that.

"Really the end," Bert said finally. Somehow his voice had changed, and I knew that he had thought of Brooks and Rob not being there and of Phil, who would have said something, away at Lakeview. "Yeah, if you don't do it we'll really murder you, string you right up."

I thought the best thing to do was keep talking. "I'm not sure this is going to work, but I can probably put on some kind of act."

"That's better," Bert said.

"How long do you think it'll take you to get all this together?" I asked, thinking that Brooks and Rob should be around for the weekend.

"Maybe tomorrow if everything looks all right. It depends on the girls. They've got to be some place close to the barn because you have to make it happen fast."

"Tomorrow?" I lost hope.

"That's right," Bert said. "I've got a rope down at the store, so we could wander over there and measure it. First Rusty and I'll go get it and you guys wait here."

When they got back we started over, seeing no one as we went past the house and into the barn. Bert brought the rope out from under his shirt. He tied a slip knot and then went up the ladder after arranging the loop at its base.

"Anyone can see that," Rusty said.

"Just wait," Bert said, starting down after looping the end of the rope around the top of the ladder. Shavings and dry corn husks littered the floor by the Liberty Six. Bert did a thorough job of covering the loop.

"You going to leave it there?" I asked.

"Hell, no. This is just to practice. Now everyone up into the loft except for you, Tom."

"Everybody quiet," he said a bit later. The giggles and grunts and puffings up above stopped. The trap door to the loft showed only a black square.

"Now, Tom," Bert called down, "you start to come up the ladder too."

"I thought I was to get the girls here," I protested.

"Just shut up and start up the ladder," Bert said, and again his voice had that full, fierce tone in it.

I stepped over to the ladder and had my right foot on the first rung before I understood, too late, what was going on. I felt the rope coming up over my hips, and I made the mistake of bringing my arms down off the ladder, because if I hadn't done that the noose would have slid right up and over my hands. I wasn't really caught yet, but I knew I'd better be. As I let the rope tighten, I said, "Wow, Bert, you really got me that time!"

That turned out to be the right thing to say. As Bert and Rusty and the rest came tumbling down the ladder they were all so pleased at Bert's tricking me that they left me alone. For a minute I'd been afraid they would really tie me up, but while everyone was telling Bert what a swell plan it was I eased off a little, loosening the rope around my chest and sliding it over my head.

"See, it really works!" Bert said. "I guess I can still show you high-class buggers something, after all."

I realized he was really talking about Brooks and Rob, and maybe even Phil. Me, too, in a way. I knew I must be learning something because I kept still and didn't say that I'd never thought of being high-class and that Fran said we were straight middle class. But I could tell that saying that meant a lot to Bert. He hid the rope under his shirt again. I hoped I could get away and began drifting off toward the screened back porch of the house.

Then Bert called out, "Hey, Tom, hold up."

I turned and walked back to the group because I didn't want to bring them any closer to the house.

Bert said, "Remember, it's on for tomorrow if the girls are close enough."

"Who's supposed to be hurt, anyway?" I asked.

"We'll figure that out," he said. "Hell, *I'll* be the hurt one—a bad fall in the loft, the pitchfork getting me in the crotch." He grabbed himself between his legs and laughed and the others laughed too. "That'll bring the girls running," he said. "So you remember, Tom."

"I'll remember."

They went on around the house and out into the street. No one seemed to care that I didn't follow them. I went back into the barn and collected the horseshoes. I stood at one stake and pitched all four shoes at the other. Then I trudged over, collected the shoes, and pitched them back. I got tired of this after a while, but I didn't want to go into the house. I hung the horseshoes up in the barn. I walked over to the ladder and climbed up through the trap door, closing it after me before I sat down on the straw-covered boards. I looked out through the ventilator slats toward Main Street. No one was around. The whole town looked dead and I wished I was dead, too.

I wondered where the girls would be. For a few wild moments I thought of just leaving a note in my alcove for Mother and setting out for Lakeview. I'd have to walk all night, which might not be too bad, but I didn't know where the Creightons were staying.

What bothered me more than anything else was what might happen to Martha or whatever other girl got captured. Bert's talk about getting hurt in the crotch and the snickering comments of

Rusty and some of the others worried me. I wasn't quite as innocent as they seemed to think I was and a lot of lurid pictures of what could happen came to me there in the half light of the loft.

I don't know how long I brooded up there before I heard voices. Fran and Heidi appeared and went into the house. After a while I saw Heidi alone, walking slowly down to the street. A few moments later Mrs. Hauser came out. Heidi stopped and waited for her mother to catch up and I knew they were on their way back to the old caboose.

I began to think about Fran. We didn't see each other as often as we did in Shanghai and I missed her. The more I thought about this the more I felt it wouldn't be a bad idea to see if I couldn't talk to Fran right now, because there had to be at least another half hour before supper.

After walking around to the front door I went upstairs and found Fran in the bedroom. Before I could say anything she asked, "Do you know what Heidi Hauser has done?" and I could tell she was angry.

"No, what?"

"She's wearing just for everyday those good clothes I gave her, the underwear with the eyelet embroidery and all that."

"I didn't know you'd given her any clothes," I said.

"You didn't?" She sounded both surprised and annoyed. "You haven't been paying much attention to anything, I guess. It was partly for Mrs. Hauser's cleaning the walk. Mother and I talked it over and gave the things to Heidi. But they're not just everyday things, you know."

This didn't sound important to me, but I saw I'd have to wait. "I'd better get cleaned up," I said.

"Yes, you're really a mess," she said.

I went to the bathroom and washed off. Back in my alcove I put on a clean shirt. Fran was still frowning when I stepped into the big bedroom, but at least she'd stopped talking about Heidi.

"Do you know where the girls are going to be tomorrow?" I asked.

"Martha thought we might meet here early in the afternoon," Fran said, "and then maybe go down and try swimming under the tracks down the line. What difference would it make to you?"

"Quite a bit," I said, looking away from her.

"The part in your hair is crooked," she said, "and too far to the right. What's the matter with you, anyway? Are you getting an attack of asthma?"

"I wish I was," I said, thinking of the luxury of lying in bed, gasping for air.

"You really are loony," she said. "Listen, they're already forgetting about the walnuts. How could we have known anything about that to begin with?"

"I'm not thinking about the walnuts."

"They're the real reason I gave those nice hand-embroidered things to Heidi."

I knew she'd be off on that again if I didn't stop her. "I'm afraid Martha or one of the other girls may get hurt tomorrow."

That stopped her. "You must be getting something worse than asthma," she said. "Brain fever, perhaps."

I knew she didn't mean that, but I said, "Could be."

"What is it, Tom?"

"I'm afraid to tell anyone, even you," I said. Then she wasn't angry any more. She came over to me and took hold of my left shoulder. "If you're in a mess you'd better tell me. Has anyone been talking to you?"

"Bert Kratz says he'll kill me if I don't do what he wants," I said.

"I suppose he needs some more money for that tacky clubhouse."

"It's worse than that."

"I can't help you, Tom, unless you tell me."

"No one can help me," I said.

Fran shook my shoulder. "Tom, sometimes you are a complete idiot."

"Promise not to tell?"

"Of course not," she said. "I'll make up my own mind when I know what it is."

I spilled it all out except I didn't say anything about Bert getting a pitchfork in his crotch.

Fran let go of my shoulder. "Let's sit on the bed while I think," she said. We sat on the bed and I waited. After a while she said, "Even if it worked on *you*, I don't think it would work on Martha—she's bigger and pretty strong. And then, nothing much could really happen, you know."

"Bert and Rusty said something about holding her hostage and making her kiss them."

"*Kiss* them?" Fran said, her lip going up. "More likely they think they could lift up her skirt."

"Fran!" I said, dismayed.

"Don't put on that know-nothing act for *me*, Tom," she said.

"Well, all right," I said, "but still . . . "

"Listen," she said, "I won't tell anyone but Martha. You go right ahead tomorrow and put on your best act. Martha's no fool."

"What if she doesn't get there first?"

"Either she or I will get there first," Fran declared.

"Oh, Fran!" I felt fear and relief. I was afraid I was going to cry, but I knew that would disgust Fran completely.

Mother's voice at the door saved me. We hadn't heard her coming upstairs. "Children, you'll be late if you don't hurry," she said.

"We're ready," Fran said smoothly as we stood up. "Tom and I got to talking about living in Dalton and all the things we're learning."

"How nice," Mother said. "I must say you both seem to be fitting in very well."

As we followed Mother downstairs Fran looked at me with her lips pursed and I answered by crossing my eyes.

10 🐚

I REACHED SIOUX FALLS even earlier than I'd hoped. At a filling station I went to the pay phone and took out a handful of change. The operator put my call through to Dalton. After a couple of rings I heard "Hello?" in what was so recognizably Martha's voice that I couldn't speak for a moment. "Hello? Hello?" she repeated, and I heard myself saying inanely, "Martha, it's really you, isn't it? I mean, you're really there in Dalton, aren't you?"

"Where else?" she said, laughing. "Why would you call me, Tom, if you didn't think I was here?"

"I know I sound confused," I said, "but at least you know who I am."

"Why, Tom Jerome, I'd know your voice anywhere, any time."

"Really?"

"Oh, really," she said, reminding me of Brooks imitating me long ago. "But just where are you?"

"Sioux Falls," I said. "I should be coming in late this afternoon."

"Wonderful!" Martha said. "All the way from Sioux Falls—you're sure?"

"The road's been fine," I said, "and the forecast from Omaha is clear."

"If Bert were here he might give you a shortcut," she said. "He's had to drive up to Lakeview to track down an order for the store that got sent to the wrong place, but he'll be back. We'll wait dinner for you."

The operator broke in, and Martha said, "Just hang up, Tom, and come right along." The line went dead before I could tell her not to wait.

Even if I hadn't already been thinking about Bert's plan to trap Martha, her voice would have thrown me back to that disastrous afternoon in Dalton. The boys began to drift over to the clubhouse. I felt sick, waiting under the locusts by the barn and keeping an eye on the corner of the clubhouse lot down the road. When I saw Bert coming from the direction of Main Street, Rusty and some of the others with him, I knew I had to move.

I tried to look casual as I strolled out, kicking up a bit of dust. I wasn't sure any longer that I should have told Fran because there was a good chance Bert would flub the job.

"You know where the girls are?" Bert demanded as I came up to the group.

"They're meeting on the lawn the other side of our house," I said.

"That's real lucky," Rusty said.

"We've got to make up a reason for going to the barn," Bert said.

"They couldn't see us if we circle around the other side," I said, thinking that the faster this went the better for me.

"The Chink's right," Bert said, "and anyway, we go into the Lloyd barn often enough."

I knew better than to say that we went in only when Brooks or Rob was there. I could see they all thought of me as being a Lloyd.

"We'd better start," Bert said. "You can't tell about women. They might decide to go somewhere and we'd have to set up everything all over again."

I thought it was funny to hear him say "women."

We started off, passing the side of the house, circling under the locust trees to go behind the barn and coming around to the front and into the darkness.

I could just catch a glimpse of Fran's striped pink and white linen skirt beyond the corner of the house. That meant she and Martha had sat down closest to the barn. I knew that ought to make me feel better, but it didn't.

Inside the barn, Rusty and Bert and the others began to talk a little and laugh at their own dumb jokes. Rusty started up the ladder to the loft.

"You might as well stay down here, Tom," Bert said, arranging the noose.

"Are you still the one who's supposed to be hurt?"

"Sure, why not?" He looked up at me.

"I just have to know. I can't go running over to the girls for help just saying *someone's* hurt, can I?" I heard the tone in my voice and knew I wasn't doing myself any good.

"Probably not," Bert said. Rusty called down to know if he should begin tightening the rope and swing it behind one side of the ladder.

"Not yet," Bert called back, scuffing some more shavings and dust over the noose.

Satisfied, he straightened up. "Sure, I'm the one to be hurt, and you tell it to *Martha,* see?"

"That's right," Rusty said above us. "Tell her Bert's run the pitchfork right through his balls."

"You bet," Bert said, spreading his legs and rubbing himself while Rusty snickered up in the loft. Bert climbed the ladder with a swaggering swing of his fat buttocks under his overalls and went through the trap door. He looked down, tested the rope, and said, "All right, Tom. You put on a good act, Chinky, or you'll be sorry for the rest of your short life."

There was nothing for it now, so I began loping across the back yard and speeded up half way, shouting, "Oh! Oh! We need *help!*" as I rounded the corner. Almost crashing into Fran, I made my voice quiver as I said, " Help! Bert's hurt himself terribly in the loft! Oh please, *please* come!" I rolled my eyes and panted.

Fran jumped up almost too fast. Martha showed better control, but she was on her feet too now. The other girls had just looked up, surprised, and I could see Heidi at the far end looking scared.

"Bert?" Martha said. "What's happened?"

"He's hurt in the loft," I gasped out. "He got caught with a pitchfork."

"A pitchfork? How?" Martha asked.

"Between his legs," I blurted out, "in his crotch!"

As Martha started to run toward the barn with me and Fran behind her, I knew she was teasing me as she called out, "My, my! Between his legs—what a clumsy thing to do!" and her tone almost gave her away. She was streaking across the yard now and Fran and I could scarcely keep up with her.

As we ran into the barn I said, "In the loft! He's in the loft. I hope he hasn't bled to death!"

"Poor Bert!" Martha said, as if she really felt pity for him. "We've got to get to him."

She'd reached the bottom of the ladder and as she cried out "Oh, oh!" I saw her looking carefully at the boards. "I'm going right up," she said loudly then, and as she did the rest of the girls began to come into the barn behind us.

Martha put her right foot on the lowest rung of the ladder. She reached out with her left hand before she took hold of the left upright and circled the rope together with it. As she took her next step Bert must have pulled on the rope to bring up the noose. Martha screamed, "Something's burning my hand! It's a *snake!*"

She stopped climbing. The noose came up, almost catching her legs, but she was ready and jumped back down, holding on to the rope shouting, "No, it's a rope moving, not a snake! Oh, poor Bert must be strangling!"

She took hold of the rope with both hands and jerked it hard.

At the word "snake" some of the girls had run out of the barn. I saw Heidi standing just inside the door looking on, not taking part in any of it. Martha must have timed her jerk just right because there was a bang against the trap door and Bert said, "Oh, crap!"

Martha called up, "Bert, Bert, are you strong enough to reach the door? There's a rope down here I almost got tangled in. Should we get Dr. Chapman? Quick, Tom, you'd better run down to Main Street and see if he's in."

Naturally, Bert couldn't let that happen, so he stuck his head out, his face flushed. "No, no, Martha, don't do that! I'm all right."

"I'll come up and see," Martha said, taking hold of the ladder again. "Have you lost a lot of blood?"

Bert's fat rump filled the open space above the ladder as he started down, saying, "It was just a trick, Martha, just to have a little fun, you know. Nobody's hurt. We just thought there ought to be a little excitement around town."

Martha kept it up as if she hadn't heard him. "But the pitchfork! Why, Tom said you got it in your *crotch!*" She stepped right up to him and put her hand between his legs. He backed off, stumbling, then lost his balance and fell. Martha went down beside him, her hand on him. "Why, you aren't even bloody!" she said.

I glanced at Fran. She had her lip up.

Then I hadn't time to think about that because Martha, after giving Bert a last pat, harder than before, making him say "Easy!" jumped up, whirled around and came to me, swinging the rope.

"So you came and *lied* to us, Tom! What a dirty trick to play!"

I saw she had to do something like this and that I couldn't just stand there as if the whole thing had ended. I couldn't say I'd been bullied into it, so I grinned as I turned and said, "I guess I fooled you all right," and started to run. She swung the rope end and missed me the first time, but as I got to the barn door I had to sidestep to get around Heidi, and Martha caught me a smart lick right across the back of my knees.

It didn't sting all that hard, but I let out a yelp and made it across the back yard in a hurry. I could hear everyone behind me laughing, and I decided Martha felt she'd done enough because I couldn't hear her any longer. I turned around the house and went in through the front door and upstairs to the bathroom, which I needed. I didn't feel too bad about the whole thing just then. In fact, I thought I'd been pretty lucky.

𝑒❧ 11

AND THEN I was coming into Dalton in the dead of winter. The Chevy's tires thudded across the railroad tracks. Looking south, I saw the grain elevator Uncle Fred had managed for a while after that summer. Even in the failing evening light I could see it stood rusting, unused. And now I was turning into Main Street. It looked much the same, with the high curb by Fenton's Market, a holdover from the days when wagons unloaded at the store level. Maybe they still unloaded that way from trucks.

I drove down the two business blocks between the modest façades of a couple of law offices. I'd already noticed the gas pump in the front of Fenson's. Next to it came KRATZ & SON—*General Store.* And then on my right, in the second block, I saw the front of the old bank building, the gilt letters still on the plate glass window—COM-MERCIAL BANK OF DALTON—scratched and peeling. I remembered that the property had come down to Aunt Netty after Grandma Tessy's death, but it hadn't occurred to me that it would still be standing there.

Turning right, I drove slowly down the next two blocks and there ahead, where the street ended, and just a trifle out of line with the end of the street, stood the old Lloyd house. Against the snow, the painted wood took on an ivory glow, accented by the failing light, as if it drew what color it could from the setting sun.

I looked at the two tall, leafless walnut trees still flanking the walk. I had been prepared for everything to look diminished, the house not so large and imposing as I had remembered it, the distances shrunken, but the place appeared much the same—solid and well kept. The middle upstairs bedroom, Grandma Tessy's, jutted out over the entrance, just as I remembered it.

I was about to make the turn and park in front of the walk, when the front door opened and there against the light came a solid figure that could only be Bert's, waving his arms like a cop directing traffic. I saw that he wanted me to take the new driveway, leading almost directly off the street to the old barn, where it curved. I drove in through the open barn door and parked the Chevy beside what must be Bert's chartreuse Cadillac.

Then Bert himself came lumbering down the drive.

"Well, Tom," he said, with the exact tone of heartiness I knew he would have, a heartiness that I couldn't feel was genuine, sounding like a parody of the Knellers' greetings. "Well, Tom, old man," he said, "you made if after all. You must have grown a heavy foot."

"Yeah, I really floored the pedal for the last hundred," I said, easing gratefully into this particular all-American exchange. Gratefully, because I felt my old dislike of him returning.

"Martha'll sure be glad to see you," he said. "She's been worrying. Here, let me carry something."

"I've got it all," I said, but Bert grabbed my briefcase, saying, "Come on, Tom, that's no way to be," and I felt the familiar rage rising in me. I fought it down as well as I could, telling myself that all that had happened long ago.

We went up to the back porch, enclosed in glass now, with a storm door added. In the service area a washing machine stood, its lid open. We stepped around a dryer to get to the kitchen door.

"Tom!" Martha called out as we stepped inside. She came toward me, arms open. As we hugged and kissed I remembered how overwhelmed I'd been that summer by all the physical affection. At home we weren't a particularly demonstrative family, and I still found it hard to believe that anyone was really that happy to see me or felt so sincerely a claim to kinship.

But there it all was, and the steamy kitchen, with its smell of food cooking, threw me back to the heat of summer.

"Martha!" I said, trying to respond with a warmth equal to hers. "It's great to get here."

"We weren't sure you'd make it," she said. "You know, you were so impractical and foreign as a kid that it's hard to think you could pilot yourself all the way from California to Wyoming and on to Dalton."

That too threw me back into the summer. I rallied and said, "Believe me, I'm an old touring hand by now." I could see that they still thought of me as the scrawny cousin from China.

"Bert'll take you up to your room," Martha said. "I thought you'd like to have the same one, but all to yourself this time, and you won't have to sleep in that little alcove because it's gone."

"That's great," I said.

"And Bert," she went on, "while you're upstairs see if you can't find those wild new pajamas of yours." She came close to giggling. "Can you believe it, Tom, that Bert, at his age, came home a few weeks ago with a pair of wine-colored silk pajamas?"

Bert, paunchy and heavy bottomed, paused and turned, looking sheepish. "I thought they were a good buy," he said, "a real bargain."

"Wine-colored, Tom, and with blue piping," Martha went on, not letting him off. "And they *were* a bargain, but only because they aren't color-fast. Made in Japan, I bet. I have to do them with the rags, and that's why I need them now, to finish the load."

I wondered if Martha had deliberately thrown in Japan for my benefit, wondered if she sensed that I really was still the China boy in many ways.

"I must have tossed them into a corner of my closet," Bert said. "I'll have a look around. Come on, Tom."

"I'm surprised Martha remembers what room I slept in," I said as we went upstairs. "That was more than twenty years ago."

"Martha remembers everything," Bert said. "I keep telling her, forget it, don't try to hold on to so much. But she's just like Dalton, you know. Here," he said, opening a door and going in ahead of me to turn on a light. "If it wasn't for the old store I'm not sure I'd stay here, but it's still the best house for miles around, the way it always was. You know, I've got a branch over in Carlton, and the branch is bigger than Pop's old store here. I might even open another up in Lakeview. Those towns are moving."

"I was surprised to see the bank with the same old sign. It looked deserted."

"Well, Netty wants it kept that way, even though it's my building now," Bert said. "I use it for storage, you know."

"Good idea," I said, even though I recoiled from the idea of Bert Kratz using Grandfather Lloyd's building that way.

"You can see we've fixed up the place," he said, opening another door. "We've got a bathroom for you here—divided the old alcove dressing rooms, put in a stall shower, really made the place up to date."

"I can see," I said. But I could also see the old room with the narrow bed for me on the other side of the wall and the big bed where Mother and Fran had slept. I tried to feel neutral about the changes, tried to make no judgments. What Martha and Bert did with the Lloyd house shouldn't be any of my affair. I tried to fight back my old feeling about Bert, telling myself that was all past, that he was Martha's husband, a settled, dull, small businessman, grown pudgy, who would end up fatter and flabbier than his father had been. I stood taller than Bert now; I could physically look down on him, and this obvious fact became ridiculously important to me.

He stood waiting at the door. "I'll be down in just a couple of minutes," I said. "And don't forget those pajamas."

"Yeah, sure," he said.

As I started down in a few minutes, Martha appeared at the foot of the stairs. "I hope you won't mind eating in the kitchen."

"Where else?" I said. "Just like old times."

"Then you remember?"

"I remember everything," I said, "but not all the time."

"Let me show you the living room," she said as Bert joined us. "You remember how sacred it was."

I looked at the flowered chintz and the overstuffed chairs. At least it was comfortable. "It'll be a few minutes before we eat," Martha said. As I sank into a chair I intercepted a glance between them. "It's funny to think that we're cousins but we don't know each other all that well. Actually, Tom, I'm babbling along like this trying to get up the nerve to ask if you'd like something before dinner."

"I see what you mean," I said. "You're thinking of the frail mission boy and all that. I'd like a good shot of scotch, neat, if that's convenient."

"Well, thank God for that!" Bert brought out with his grating heartiness. "I'm a sour mash man myself, and I've converted Martha."

Martha smiled. "Bert was so worried—said we'd have to sneak our drinks on the sly."

"What a pain I must have been that summer for everyone," I said. "Uncle Drew and Uncle Fred were always finding excuses for going out to the barn, and once or twice I wondered about Grandma Tessy."

"You remember that too?" Martha asked as we waited for Bert to come back. "I think Old Lady Hauser was her supplier."

"I hadn't thought of that," I said. "I suppose she kept it under her mattress along with her money roll."

Bert came back with a tray.

"You knew about her stash of bills?" Martha asked, surprised.

My answer was cut off by Bert's saying, "Here I am, serving the Lloyds as usual," with something close to pride in his voice. I saw it wasn't serving us that pleased him, but that we were together as equals.

"The Lloyds haven't exactly changed the world or even held together much," I said, "except for thinking about Wyoming, and now that'll soon be over."

"That's right," Martha said. "We'll finish it all in probate court tomorrow in Center City."

"That soon?" I asked.

"I called Aunt Netty up in Edina after you phoned," she said. "She and Uncle Carl will meet us tomorrow. But of course you must come back and stay as long as you can."

"A lot depends on the weather," I said. "I have to be back in L.A. for the new semester."

"What a long way to drive just for this," Martha said.

"I know," I said. "But I've always liked to drive and it's been good to get away for a while by myself. And then, sometimes I try to pretend that Dalton is my home town, the place you have to go back to to find yourself."

"You're sure as hell welcome to it," Bert said.

"Is anyone I know left here besides the two of you? What about Rusty Blair and Phil Creighton—and Heidi Hauser?"

"Rusty was killed in the war," Bert said matter-of-factly. "The Creightons moved to Des Moines and somebody told me a long time ago that Phil went to Drake and on to law school. With that smart mouth of his he ought to be doing pretty well."

"And I think Heidi became a secretary in Center City after business college," Martha said. "Then I think she moved over to Lakeview for some kind of job in one of the entertainment franchises.

"Yeah," Bert said, "Lakeview's grown a lot recently—left places like Dalton behind."

"Her mother saved Fran and me about those walnuts," I said.

"What a fuss over nothing!" Martha said.

"I don't know about that," Bert said, as if *his* property could have suffered severe damage. "It was a real dumb thing for you two to do."

"It was," I said, trying to keep my voice neutral.

Martha got up to go to the kitchen. And there I was with Bert. I wondered what he thought of me now. His eyes kept looking past me. I took another swallow of scotch and heard myself saying, "Sitting here is like sitting in two rooms, isn't it? I can still see the horsehair sofa and the bamboo étagère at the same time as I see this new bright room. Whatever happened to that miniature bale of cotton from the Chicago Fair?"

"What?"

"You know," I said. "All that étagère's collection of bric-à-brac. As a kid I lusted after that bale of cotton."

Martha overheard me as she came back. "When we took over the house Netty got all that kind of thing."

"I wouldn't remember," Bert said stiffly and I realized that for all I knew Bert Kratz might never have seen the front sitting room as it was, and with my attempt at polite conversation I had probably antagonized him all over again. At the same time, it went a long way toward turning this living Bert, fleshy, banal, into the younger Bert of the jabbing hands, the bully, envious of the Lloyds, challenging Brooks and Rob.

He had triumphed in some way on his own terms. He lived in the Lloyd house. He had married Martha. And Martha? She seemed happy enough. I wondered why there were no children, but that wasn't any business of mine.

As we went out to eat, Martha said, "Did you turn up those pajamas?"

"No," Bert said. "You sure you didn't pick them up yourself?"

"I'd almost certainly remember," Martha said, "you big romantic booby, but I ought to start that wash, so you two sit down and I'll be right back." This was domesticity with a vengeance, I thought. I knew I should be pleased that Martha could talk with such easy intimacy in front of me, but I couldn't think of anything to say because I had a hilarious vision of Bert's bulk encased in wine-colored silk. So I concentrated on my second scotch as Bert gulped his sour mash. I heard the sound of water going into the washing machine, and then Martha was back with us, serving us dinner and asking questions.

"What kind of house do Aunt Emma and Uncle Gordon live in?" she demanded. I must have looked puzzled because it took me a moment to realize that she was asking me about Mother and Father.

"I didn't know whom you meant, it's been so long since I've heard them called that. They live in a regular California redwood bungalow in Pasadena," I said. "Amy and the girls and I get over to see them as often as we can manage."

"It's nice they're so close to you," she said. "Dad and Mom keep talking about leaving Des Moines and the cold winters and moving away, but I don't know if they'll ever do it."

I knew I couldn't say it wasn't always convenient to have your parents just around the corner, but with Martha's questions and my answers and Bert's occasional remarks about business and Dalton and the Lloyds and Lakeview, we made it through the meal. I came to understand that I wasn't especially curious about the new Dalton I'd returned to, that it was still the old Dalton I had to deal with, but we sat for almost an hour in the new front room, looking at old pictures, and I showed them pictures of Amy and Maude and Mary. As I did this, I began to look forward to calling home in the morning, to asking how everything had been going since I'd left.

"You're lucky to have the children," Martha said.

Before I could say anything Bert, with surprising conviction said, "I don't know. It's a crazy world for kids to grow up in nowadays."

"Wasn't it always?" I heard myself saying, and even as I spoke I thought I should have kept my mouth shut.

When neither of them spoke I got up, stretching, and said, "I know you won't think me rude when I say I'm tired. It's been a long drive and if we're actually going right up to Center City tomorrow to settle everything I'd better get to bed."

"Should I call you in the morning?" Martha asked.

"Yes, please," I said, "especially if we have a regular time to meet Aunt Netty."

"I'll wake you if you aren't down by nine."

When I was ready for bed I found myself standing in what had been my old alcove. One day, when I'd begun to forget about my betrayal of Bert's plan to capture Martha, Fran said, "Let's go upstairs for a bit and talk." I followed her as she went right past the big double bed and entered the alcove, where she sat down on the edge of my cot, as if she wanted to make sure we were as alone as possible.

"What is it?" I asked, sitting beside her.

"Bert Kratz knows you told me about his trap for Martha," Fran said. "I thought you ought to know."

I felt scared, but even so, I said, "Brooks and Rob are around a good bit more these days."

"I wouldn't count on anything, Tom," she said.

"I don't see how Bert can know for sure," I said. "Only you and Martha and I know for sure."

"That's right," Fran said, "and you know *I* would never tell."

I looked straight at her for what seemed a long time. Then I said, "Martha?" and she nodded.

"But I told just so Martha wouldn't be hurt, so that Bert couldn't . . . "

"I know," she said, "but you saw how Martha took it. You really don't know very much, Tom."

"You keep telling me that," I said, "but you don't always help me."

"Well, how could *I* have known?" she asked. "I can see *now* that Martha might have liked the whole idea."

"*Liked* it?"

"Well, it's flattering, isn't it, to have someone pay that much attention to you?"

"But he talked about—I thought he was going to . . . "

"Well?" Fran said. I felt myself turning a little sick.

"I suppose I'll get beaten up," I said.

"I doubt if anything quite like that can happen to you."

"What else *could* happen to me?"

"I really couldn't say," Fran said, suddenly turning all grown up on me. "I just thought I ought to tell you."

And there I was. Sometimes I wished I'd put the plug nickel in the collection plate that first Sunday, but then I would remind myself that I hadn't had it with me in church. Then I would wish I hadn't said anything about it to anyone or had thrown it into one of the mudholes by the railroad tracks. And then again I would tell myself that I'd given it away, but I knew that I really hadn't.

I found Mother upstairs arranging some clothes in one of the bureau drawers.

"You've been looking a little tired and worried," she said as I came in. "You aren't having any asthma, are you?"

"No," I said. I thought there was nothing for it by now so I said, "I'm afraid I've done something terribly bad."

"Oh, Tom!" she said, turning to face me.

"Do you remember the money Mr. Carter gave me?"

"Of course," she said. "It's yours to do with as you wish."

"I gave most of it for the clubhouse," I said. "I know they let me into the club because I have my allowance and I'm not worried about that, because Brooks and Rob have been very decent to me. But finally I gave away the plug nickel, not really gave it away, though. We spent it at Kratz's for candy, and Mr. Kratz didn't even look at it or ring it."

"You mean that nickel that Joe Carter made his silly joke about?"

"What joke?" I asked.

"Didn't he say something about its being a plug nickel?"

"Yes, and that's the problem," I said.

Mother began to laugh and then stopped. "You mean you took him seriously? That's just an old comic phrase by now. There may have been a time when it was worth counterfeiting a nickel, but only long ago. And wherever would someone like Joe Carter get a piece of false money? Oh, Tom!"

"You mean it was just a regular old nickel all the time?" I demanded.

"Of course," she said. "Really, Tom . . ." and I knew she was trying not to hurt my feelings but still had to try hard not to laugh. I felt relief for a moment but it shifted right into anger and from anger to rage.

I made for the door. "Wait, Tom, wait!" Mother said, starting to follow me, but I ran into the hall and down the stairs out through the kitchen, half-hearing Mrs. Hauser say something about corncobs. I dashed across the back porch and down the steps, crossing the horseshoe pitch at full speed and entered the darkness of the barn. I climbed up into the loft, closed the hatch after me and sat there, leaning against mildewed hay.

I don't know how long I hid there until I heard sounds, voices of both girls and boys. The old division had begun to break down. No one talked any more about finishing the clubhouse.

After listening for a while without being able to make out any words, I got up and went over and opened the hatch door. I climbed down the ladder slowly, still full of being cheated over the nickel and angry and afraid of what I would have to pay for betraying Bert Kratz's plot.

I leaned against one side of the barn door. The Creightons had come back from Lakeview and, after a while, Phil happened to look over and noticed me.

He came over and said quietly, "Gee, Tom, I'm afraid you're in a mess."

"I know," I said.

"I can't think of any way to help you."

Heidi Hauser saw us then. She was standing close to Bert Kratz and said something to him. He looked over at us and then bent over, pretending he was vomiting.

I couldn't see Fran or Martha anywhere.

Then Heidi said loudly, "Look at Chinky Tom—he's skinnier than ever."

That tore it for me. Stepping out away from Phil I yelled, "Don't you dare say that or call me that, Heidi Hauser!" My shrill voice stopped everyone. Bert made a move toward me but stopped when I said, close to screaming, "Don't say that, and don't talk to me, Heidi! You wear special charity underwear for everyday. Hauser is a German name. Your mother lives in a smelly caboose without your father, whoever he is. Why don't you and your mother go back and live with the Kaiser, the Kaiserin and all the little Kaiserettes?"

Somebody snickered.

I knew I was doomed and the only person there I could attack was Heidi, but I already felt sick, thinking of Mrs. Hauser's hands dipped in lye to save me.

The pain started in Heidi's eyes. She looked up at Bert, reaching toward him, but he had backed away.

I couldn't stand any more. With tears starting in my own eyes I ran back through the hushed group into the house and up to the alcove, where I lay face down on the cot.

12 🐦

I woke early that first winter morning back in Dalton and came downstairs in my dressing gown to find Bert talking over something with Martha in the kitchen, a note of complaint and injustice in his voice.

"You'd think by now they'd have got things straight," he was saying when he caught sight of me. "There you are, Tom. Another shipment to the old store here hasn't shown up. I don't know how many times it's happened. But if it isn't too much trouble for you, we'll go to Center City in two cars. You can drive Martha and I'll see if I can't track things down. If it isn't the express company dummies, it's the stupid railway guys who're always messing up. Of course, Dalton hasn't been anything but a whistle stop for years, but you'd think they'd learn."

"That's fine with me," I said.

"And anyway," Bert went on as we sat down to orange juice and coffee, "you don't need *me* at the court for probate. *I'm* not a Lloyd, after all."

"Nor a Jerome, lucky man," I said, doing my best to assume my friendliest smile.

"Certainly not," he said. "Wouldn't that be something—to be part Chinese the way you are!"

"At least it's a good act," I said. "You know, until I finally settled in California I always thought of myself as a Middle Westerner."

Bert almost choked on his orange juice. "*You? A Midwesterner?* That's a good one, isn't it, Martha? My God, Tom, you're about as Midwestern as a Mandarin!"

"Oh, I don't know," Martha said. "Tom always managed to fit in."

Bert's Mandarin remark stunned me. I'd never thought of him as capable of anything like that. He returned to his theme before I could speak. "Anyway, *I'm* not a Lloyd, and you can wrap everything up without me if I can't make it in time."

He sounded both proud and resentful. Proud, I supposed, because he had married into the Lloyds and resentful, perhaps, because Brooks and Rob, the "Lloyds" of his youth, had never given in to him.

"You always carry on so about the Lloyds, Bert," Martha was saying.

"Well, the old man was really somebody," Bert said.

"It was a long time ago," she said as she got up to serve us our bacon and eggs.

"You've certainly brightened up this room," I said.

"Yeah, we really have," Bert said. He had been eating rapidly. "Look, you two, take your time. I don't know how long I'll be tracking down that shipment. I'll try to get to the courthouse, but don't count on it."

Bert got up. "Make certain to check your car, Tom. There's a cold front—snow almost for sure—coming down from the north. You're sure as hell not in sunny Southern California, you know."

I felt about nine years old again. I wanted to say I'd got this far on my own, but instead I did my best to keep my voice cordial. "Thanks for the warning."

After Bert left, Martha poured us each another cup of coffee. "There's really no hurry, Tom. It takes no time at all to get to the courthouse. Bert's always in such a hurry to get things done."

I wondered what it had been like for her to be married all these years to Bert Kratz. I knew I couldn't ask. I hadn't even known Martha well enough that summer to understand why she hadn't resented—had even, I supposed now—enjoyed Bert's great capturing plan.

She sat there easily, comfortably. "You should have brought Amy and the girls," she said. "I know we're not much of a family any more in the way our mothers thought of family, but it's still something to hold to."

"I suppose," I said. "I thought we might make a family trip of it myself, but Amy thought I should come alone, that it was *my* past and not any part of hers."

"What a way to talk!"

"I must call home, now that I'm here," I said. "I don't know just why, but Amy said not to call until I'd actually reached Dalton."

After I'd helped her clear the dishes, Martha wouldn't let me stay in the kitchen. "You make that call right now, Tom, from the phone in the living room. And *don't* make it *collect*. You know, seeing it on the bill will be a kind of memento of your being here—the closing of the estate."

I couldn't understand why she felt so strongly about this, but I didn't argue. Settled in the bright new living room, I got through to California.

"How are you?" Amy asked immediately.

"Fine, fine," I said. "Why wouldn't I be?"

"Oh, don't try to be coy about it," she said, laughing. "You know perfectly well that whenever you talk about that summer in Dalton and the Lloyds and all the rest your voice actually changes."

"Well, in China I *was* a boy soprano in the school quartet, but Maude and Mary are living proof that I've gone a little beyond that."

"There you go," she said. "By the way, be sure to reverse the charges on this call."

"I can't," I said. "Martha wouldn't hear of it."

"And Martha is one of your blessed Lloyds, isn't she? What a family!"

"She was just talking about family," I said. "There isn't much left around here."

"And a good thing, too, if you ask me."

I could imagine the tauntingly affectionate challenge in her eyes. "I'd make you change your expression if we were together," I said.

"Sweep me off my feet, I suppose," she said.

"That's right," I said. "After all, we could send the girls to the movies and make out on the couch."

"You *are* a fool."

"Isn't that why you married me?"

"Listen, Tom . . ."

"How are Mary and Maude? Be sure to give them my love."

"We all miss you," she said, "and we all want you to hurry back, but not until the whole business is done with. And you must promise not to mention the Wyoming acreage for at least two weeks once you're here."

"It's been that bad, has it?"

"Just leave it all behind. And listen, I don't want to run up the bill. I'll call your folks in Pasadena when we hang up and then I'll call Fran."

"Why not leave that to me?"

"Because I promised to do it, and I can also tell them that your voice still sounds quite bass."

"That's right," I said in my best Chinese falsetto.

"I love you, you idiot," she said and hung up before I could answer.

As I reached the door to the hallway, I almost bumped into Martha, who looked at me quizzically. "Sorry," I said.

"Is everything all right with Amy and the girls?" she asked.

"They're fine," I said, realizing that my high Chinese tones may have startled her.

"I'm putting a roast in the oven and setting the timer," she said as we walked towards the kitchen. "We don't need to hurry, and it's not as if old Judge Osborne wouldn't drop anything he had in hand to take care of us whenever we arrived."

I heard the old Lloyd confidence as she spoke. I wondered if Bert heard it sometimes and what he thought of it.

Once we were in the Chevy, with the heater warming it up, Martha glanced at her wristwatch. "Why don't we go part of the way by section roads and look at a little of the dead past?"

"Whatever you like," I said. " 'Look at a little of the dead past' sounds like nostalgia or poetry or something."

"Whatever *you* like," she said, smiling. "Here, turn left and take the next section road right up to the first farmhouse."

A little beyond the farmhouse Martha told me to pull up on the shoulder. Across the ditch I looked at a small frame building, its two windows boarded up.

"You recognize that?" Martha asked.

"I don't think so."

"You mean they never brought you out here that summer?"

"I can't remember."

"Why, that was Grandfather Lloyd's first house in Iowa. He built it himself—just two little rooms with a fireplace. That's where he brought Grandmother, *our* grandmother, I mean, not Grandma Tessy." She sounded like Fran in the old days.

I stared at the building. Small as it was, it struck me as the product of infinite labor. A man who could build a house with his own hands—something I could never do.

"It's used as a corncrib now," Martha said. "That bothered me at first, but it's better than having it torn down."

"Who would want to do that?"

"Bert," she said. "Bert doesn't like to think of Grandfather Lloyd starting out that way, a small farmer homesteading. No, Bert wants to keep alive some great figure of a banker—a leading citizen, a leading family."

I thought I saw it, but I was afraid to ask any questions. I started up the Chevy and drove on.

"Just what *do* you remember about that summer, Tom?" Martha asked.

"Oh, almost everything," I said, turning into the highway and heading north. "But I do get mixed up sometimes about what came after. Brooks died in a car accident while I was in college, isn't that right?"

"Yes," Martha said. "I always thought that was strange, he was such a good driver, but he lost control. Rob thought he'd been drinking."

"But Kenny?" I asked. "I keep seeing him as a baby, but that's all."

"Poor Kenny!" she said. "In a way he was right at the center, wasn't he, after Aunt Floss had died? And then for him to die so young himself, after he'd gone to live with his father. Blood poisoning, just sheer carelessness. It's hard to remember how dangerous that sort of thing used to be."

I felt ashamed that I couldn't recall this, which I must have been told, but at least I knew now why I'd heard nothing of any other heirs.

Cold wind swirled in Center City Square. In the courthouse lobby Bert stood talking to a couple I knew must be Aunt Netty and Uncle Carl. Netty had the collar of her mink coat up around her neck. We kissed and then she pulled back and held me at arm's length. "Tall and dark as you are, Tom, you really do have the Lloyd look."

"Flattery will get you everywhere with me, Aunt Netty," I said. "Mother sends her love."

As I shook hands with Uncle Carl, Bert turned to Martha and said, "It's a good thing we brought two cars. It looks as if that shipment I've been worried about got shunted off to Lakeview. I've got to try and track it down. I'll just drive straight back to Dalton, with luck in time for dinner."

Netty led us down the hall to the staircase and up one flight. The door of Judge Osborne's outer office stood open and an elderly secretary greeted us. "It's hard for me to believe, Netty, that everything's going to be wound up."

"While you're doing all the winding or unwinding," Uncle Carl said, "I think I'll take a turn around the square—look at all the old sights."

Judge Osborne, coming into the outer office from his chambers, heard Uncle Carl. "I don't know how much you'll find," he said. "Center City is up and coming. If you want to find anything old you should go on down to Dalton."

"I'll take a turn, anyway," Uncle Carl said, waving to us as he stepped back into the hall. I wondered if both he and Bert felt that only Grandfather Lloyd's direct descendants should be in at this second, long delayed, death.

Perhaps even Judge Osborne had the same feeling, I thought, settling into one of three chairs waiting for us in his chambers. He went around to the other side of a large table, where what was clearly the large file of the Lloyd Estate lay ready. I handed over my own offerings: George Kneller's certified check, my power-of-attorney, the papers notarized in Wyoming. He glanced at them briefly and nodded. "Very good. This really takes care of everything, doesn't it, Netty?"

"I think it must," she said. "What a time, what a long time!"

"Still, probably not one for the record books, I imagine," he said.

Then it seemed to me that the three of us signed paper after paper. Rob, who now lived somewhere in Ohio, had sent in some notarized documents. The secretary who had received us and a younger woman she had called in kept signing as witnesses. The three of us affirmed the truth of our statements.

At last it was over. The witnesses were excused with old world courtesy by Judge Osborne, who bowed them out of the office. And then we played through an all-American scene from the past that caught me unprepared.

Judge Osborne crossed over to a cabinet that opened into a small bar. Picking up a bottle of Sandemann's five-star, he poured a wine glass each for Aunt Netty and Martha, neither of whom showed the slightest surprise.

"Rye or scotch for you, Tom?" he asked.

"Scotch, sir, if you please," I heard my most international Shanghai voice saying.

"I'm with you," he said. "Soda? Water?"

"Neat, thank you."

"Good man."

I wanted to laugh, but then I saw that we were all four standing, the others with their glasses raised and looking at me. But of course, I realized. I—good old "Chinky" Tom Jerome—was the one male there in whose veins the Lloyd blood coursed.

Raising my glass, I said, "To the memory of Thomas Drew Lloyd and the Wyoming acreage through which he has enriched us now, even as he gave us life and enriched our beings when he lived amongst us."

We all touched glasses and drank. I was not a minister's son for nothing, I thought, and I only wished that Fran could have heard me.

"That was beautiful, Tom!" Aunt Netty said, and I felt almost embarrassed to see that she was truly moved.

"Most appropriate, I must say," Judge Osborne said.

"I wasn't sure," Aunt Netty said then, "that being your father's son you would take a drink."

"Oh," I said, trying to lighten things a little, "almost all professors of English drink—it's the common road to survival."

At least Martha laughed at that and said, "Do you remember how we were told to protect poor little Tom that summer? Uncle Drew had to hide his cigars and he and Dad had to drink their hooch out behind the barn."

Aunt Netty brightened at that. "Why, I haven't heard anyone say *hooch* for ages!"

"Fran asked me if I knew what *moonshine* meant that summer," I said.

Martha snorted. "You mean you actually knew?"

"Oddly enough, I did," I said. I was on the point of saying that I'd guessed Grandma Tessy had had a bottle as well as a roll of bills under her mattress, but caught myself in time, because I didn't think that would amuse Aunt Netty, after all, and I ended lamely, "It was quite a job of protection."

After we left Judge Osborne we found Uncle Carl in the lobby. "Why don't we pick up an early lunch at the Bamboo Room of the old Mason Hotel?" Martha suggested. "Maybe I can persuade you to come on back to Dalton for the night. Remember, Judge Osborne said it was only there that you could see the old things still."

"We really must get back," Aunt Netty said. "I have a club meeting early tomorrow."

"There's something called the Bamboo Room in Center City?" I asked.

"I hadn't thought of how suitable it would be for you, Tom," Martha said. "It's a nightclubby leftover speakeasy from the early thirties."

I saw what she meant after we had crossed the square. The fake bamboo partitions of the booths glistened with black lacquer and the wallpaper reproduced the Chinese four-seasons flower scrolls.

"Really period!" I said. And Judge Osborne was right. The place was crowded with youngish businessmen and a few women. Center City hummed.

With another round of drinks in front of us—Manhattans replacing amontillado for Aunt Netty and Martha, and Uncle Carl ordering beer—and after we had ordered, Aunt Netty touched my hand, saying, "You were really there, Tom, weren't you? You really *saw* the Wyoming acreage. You must tell us about it."

Her eagerness touched me. I made the best I could out of the Knellers, the bleak rolling landscape, my jeep ride wearing the borrowed mackinaw.

"Oh, I can see it!" Aunt Netty exclaimed. "You make it so vivid! And I'm so happy that one of *us* has actually been there."

I felt the vividness must be all in her own mind. Before I had a chance to say anything, she asked, "You do think we've done the right thing, Tom?"

"The right thing?"

"Selling it, mineral rights and all, to Mr. Kneller."

This was no time for doubt. "Absolutely, Aunt Netty," I said. "You'd already done such a good job of researching, anyway, as Mother has said to me more than once." I saw that my having looked at the acreage had endowed me with an authority I hadn't the least wish to claim. For an instant I thought of mentioning how Grandfather Lloyd had come to own the land, but then I saw how cruel that would be, if Aunt Netty actually didn't know.

Instead, I said, "I'm sure there's no question about it. You know, it's both strange and familiar for me to come back. I keep telling myself that one thing I've never quite had is a real American home town, though I've tried to make Dalton into that. It doesn't always work."

"You didn't look much like a native that summer when I met you in Minneapolis," Uncle Carl said.

"I can believe that," I said. Everyone laughed and I knew we were all seeing again that spindly, wheezing kid.

"I'm afraid you still don't talk in the Dalton manner," Aunt Netty said, not critically as she might have before, but almost with a touch of jealousy. It occurred to me that her own speech had shifted a little, sometimes making her sound almost self-consciously artificial.

"No, hardly," I said.

Aunt Netty asked about Fran and I told her how Fran and Ed lived up in San Francisco with their son, and I dutifully asked about Aunt Netty and Uncle Carl's children. What a correct Oriental conversation we were having, I thought, sitting there in the Bamboo Room eating luncheon.

Once we had finished, Martha tried a last time. "You're sure you won't stay down for the night, Netty?"

"No, truly, Martha," Aunt Netty said. "I simply can't miss my club committee meeting in the morning."

"There's a roast set to go in the oven," Martha persisted, but without much force.

"I know it'll be good," Uncle Carl said, "you're such a fine cook, Martha. But there's a big cold front coming down fast, you know, even if Netty didn't have to get back."

Martha and I saw them to their Buick sedan and waved as they drove off. Once we had cleared the outskirts of Center City in the Chevy I said, "Well, that's the end of the Wyoming acreage."

"It leaves a blank, doesn't it?" she said. "It's almost as if Grandfather Lloyd had just died, finally died."

I decided not to say that not only had Grandfather Lloyd died, but all my boyhood hatred of him had died, too. I could see Grandfather Lloyd as a driven, fallible person, just like the rest of us, trying to make the best of what he had.

We said little as we drove back to Dalton. Once there, and in front of the house, I got out and opened the passenger's door for Martha. "I'm a bit restless," I said. "I think I'll take a walk through the town. It'll probably be my last walk for a long time. I hope you don't mind?"

"Of course not," Martha said as she stood in the doorway. "There's an hour or so of sunlight left. Bert ought to be back fairly soon. Don't get cold. God knows, there's nothing much to see in Dalton you haven't seen a hundred times."

"If not a hundred, at least once," I said.

I knew the time had come and I knew where I was going. I walked down the blocks to Main Street and turned into the alley running up the west side of the bank building. I walked up to the basement door. I had thought it might be locked, and if it was I was ready to force it. But the opened lock had rusted. After all, the place held nothing but ghosts now, and the door pulled open under my pressure.

I stepped inside and pulled the door shut behind me. I stood on the landing of a crude set of wooden steps without a handrail. The shadowy darkness of the place bothered me as I stepped carefully down to the dirt floor. That other day, that day in the summer when they'd brought me here had, I felt sure, been lit with a shaft of sunlight cutting across the back wall, motes of dust floating in it. Even though it was winter now, I looked for a window, a ventilator, but there wasn't anything like that. It troubled me to think that I had reworked the scene that much in my memory.

It happened the Saturday after Fran had told me Martha had let Bert know how I'd betrayed him. Brooks was back for a weekend from his farm job and Rob had the afternoon off. Everyone knew by now the clubhouse would never be finished, but sometimes it still brought the boys together. It seemed just as clear that Bert and Brooks, and maybe even Rob and Rusty had outgrown that kind of thing. They were even beginning to shave. I told myself this, as if it meant that I might get off, that I might seem so insignificant now and what I had done so unimportant that no one could stoop to punishing me. I didn't believe a word of all that, I just told it to myself in desperation. I even told myself that since the summer was more than half over Bert might forget how little time there was left, and I knew that was impossible too.

I hung around the kitchen after lunch. "Aren't you going out?" Mother said.

"It's terribly hot, maybe I'll lie down for a while," I said. Just then Rob and Phil showed up, coming around the house to the back steps. I knew they had come for me. "Say, Tom," Phil said, his voice close to breaking, "it's about time to come on over to the clubhouse."

"All right," I said, "I'm coming."

"It's nice of them to come and ask you," Mother said.

I couldn't even try to answer that.

For an instant as the three of us walked in silence toward the clubhouse I thought Phil was going to say something, but after he'd taken in his breath and held it for a while, he just let it out in a long sigh. We walked neither fast nor slow. When we got to the clubhouse everyone was there. Bert and Brooks stood apart from the others facing each other.

As the three of us came up, Bert asked, "You got the key, Brooks?"

"I've got it," Brooks said.

"You shouldn't have taken it without asking," Rob said.

"Don't be a fool," Bert said.

I could feel that Bert held an edge of authority over them both now. "Let's go," he said and led the way down toward Main Street and turned into the alley. I tried to drop back, but everyone had closed in behind me, so I was next to Bert when we got to the door. He held out his hand and Brooks passed him the key. Brooks hadn't looked directly at me all this time. I knew I couldn't blame him, that he couldn't keep me from having to pay.

Bert opened the door. He turned to me and said, "Down you go, Chinky."

"What are we doing?" I managed to ask.

"Paying a visit," Bert said. "Paying a visit to the basement of your superior grandfather's busted bank."

His hands had come up in the bullying, jabbing position. I stepped past him and, scarcely hesitating on the landing, walked slowly down. I could hear them all behind me, a rumble of foot-steps.

In the center of the dirt floor I looked around. Light from some-where struck through the rough, unfinished room. "What's in here, anyway?" I said.

"Nothing, Chinky Tom, nothing," Bert said.

I walked slowly over to a corner and turned around, feeling how strange it was that no one had spoken. As I turned I saw the others had followed me from a slight distance, and here as I stood in one corner of the squarish basement they had hemmed me in in a loose arc. Bert stood at the center. A little to one side and on his left stood Brooks and Rob and Phil. They didn't meet my eyes, but I knew that whatever could have been done for me they had done.

I wondered if Bert was going to jump me, but that seemed silly. Almost any one of them could have jumped me and beaten me up anywhere, so it was crazy to come to the bank for that. I almost hoped someone would attack me, because as I went down biting, kicking, and gouging, I would leave a mark or two. Then I had a horrible idea. Maybe they were going to make Phil and me fight. I felt sick. If that was it I wouldn't move, I'd just tell Phil to come ahead and slug away and we'd both feel terrible.

Still no one moved. Then Bert looked over at Brooks and said, "All right, now's the time. You've got to tell him."

Brooks glanced at Rob, who was staring at his feet, and then looked at me with an expression that made me think he was asking my pardon.

"Well, go on," Bert commanded. I felt like throwing up, know-ing that I had given him this hold over Brooks.

Brooks cleared his throat. He pointed above me and, his voice harsh and clear, said, "Tom, that beam above you is the one that Grandfather Lloyd hung himself from."

No one spoke, but I heard a muted inbreathing as they all stared at me. If any of them had hung back before, they didn't now, but stepped up and gaped at me in anticipation, waiting for something.

Then I knew they expected me to cry out, or just cry, or collapse in a heap. And I knew too that this was the answer to everything I thought I'd understood but hadn't—the stops, the hesitations, the short silences when I came into rooms.

Grandfather Lloyd had hanged himself. With time to think about it everything would come clear.

But there was no time now. I had no time at all. If I didn't answer I was lost, maybe lost forever. I had been protected because everyone thought I was too weak, too feeble to take this, and here they all stood, waiting to see me destroyed.

Laughter welled up in me, but I knew I couldn't show it. I tilted my head back, looking up at the beam. Then I heard my voice saying, in the crisp international accent that Fran and I shared, "Oh, it was *that* one, was it? I've never been here before, so I couldn't know just which one it was."

I heard them all breathe out, sharply. They stirred. Two or three of them stepped back. Phil sneaked a quick grin at me, his eyes shining, and Rob's head came up slowly. Bert's hands came down as he stood there, fury in his face, and as my eyes flicked over to Brooks I saw relief, perhaps even a touch of pride. Brooks and Rob and Phil knew I hadn't known, hadn't dreamed of this, but now Bert and Rusty and all the others would never know for sure.

The laughter kept welling up in me, but I knew I must hold it down. Because I had Bert now, I had him. He'd played his greatest of trumps and I had called him and the card had fallen from his fingers a clowning joker.

I stood there, holding back the laughter, and looked up again at the beam. "It isn't very high, is it?" I said.

The semicircle broke and we were just a bunch of boys again. No one was going to beat me up now because that would have made Bert's defeat even worse. The uneasy balance of authority had shifted back to Brooks and Rob.

Someone said, "I always thought there'd be a couple of safes or something like that down here."

"Oh, no, the vault's upstairs," Brooks said. "Come on over here and you can see the pilings under the cement."

Three boys started up the stairs, one of them saying something to the others that brought a snort of derision, making Bert and Rusty turn away. I walked slowly over to Phil. He punched me in the shoulder.

When everyone was back up in the alley Brooks locked the door. We should have drifted back to the clubhouse, but we were no longer a group. Brooks and Rob, talking together, sounded suddenly very old, almost grown up. Bert and his crew milled around on Main Street. So Phil and I walked back together to pitch horseshoes, just the two of us.

Standing here now in my topcoat in the chilly shadows, looking up at the dusty beam, I knew I had made this winter return not to settle the Wyoming acreage except as an excuse to face this other inheritance.

I heard Mother's voice:

"Papa—" and I thought of Grandfather Lloyd hanging throttled from the beam, his life void, his bank threatened by his easy generosity, his favorite daughter dying as she gave bloody birth to a child he could feel nothing for.

"Papa—Drew—" and I thought of Uncle Drew with all his casual charm, his cigar and his flask, living, for all I knew, a dutiful marriage, and ending it in the shabby rented room when the final blackness came upon him and he stretched out on the strange bed and put the revolver to his temple and squeezed the trigger, his heart empty.

"Papa—Drew—Gordon—" and I thought of Father, who fought his way out of the paralysis of his religious melancholia that night in the hospital room and threw himself out of the window. Yes, cast himself down from a high place because he knew he had committed the unforgivable sin of pride and placed himself outside the mercy of his Presbyterian God. I thought of him regaining consciousness, his spine and legs shattered. He must have wakened to a private hell more terrifying to me than anything I could imagine, and he had lived in it for years before he came out of that blackness to patch his life together again.

"Papa—Drew—Gordon—I mean *Tom*."

Oh yes, it was a thing to be dealt with—a time for standing aside and looking and not yielding to the black hood coming down over me. Living without life, the vision of color without color. Knowing that I had followed my private map to Dalton, thinking of Amy and Maude and Mary, thinking of my profession, thinking of parody as today's lifestyle. I stood, looking at the beam in the shadows, hearing Mother's voice, feeling the hood coming down over my head, knowing my own hands pulled it.

And I stopped them and I raised my arms, wrenching that other body out of me, thinking that I might cry out as I pulled it free. But I felt no pain, only a dizzying emptiness as I stretched out my arms holding that other body. Crossing to the corner I hung it there from the beam and backed off, my shoes scuffing the damp dirt.

Looking into the shadowy corner now I could almost see the transparent skull and brain and the inward-gazing eyes. I could almost see the hands as limp as my own now at my sides and the long limbs hanging, the pale arteries and paler veins. And through the shadows I felt the pulse of that indulgent, arrogant, self-pitying heart.

I took another step back from the corner and now only the movement of that heart remained. And in the shadows of the icy chamber I stood, and I looked until I saw no motion and I felt only the winter cold and the warm beating of my own heart.

Some time later a shaft of sunlight slanted down and I knew that it came from the door above, which had been opened. I felt a surge of joy that I hadn't been mistaken, that there had been this shaft of sunlight that summer, brighter then and at a sharper angle with the dust motes dancing, because the door had simply been left open that afternoon.

I saw the stocky legs coming down the stairs.

"Tom!" Bert called. "Tom, are you down there?"

"I'm here," I said.

He took the final steps heavily. The years fell away as I looked at his leering lips.

"I told Martha I'd find you." His voice echoed the old bullying tone.

"Yes," I said, choking back a laugh. Though the years had fallen away and I saw his hands coming up as he turned toward me at the foot of the stairs, I was not a skinny kid any more. If Bert forgot and dared to touch me, he would get my knee in his pudgy crotch. I almost wished he would forget as he moved through the space between us.

He stopped. His tongue ran out over his lips. "Tell me, Tom, old boy. Did you know—really *know* that afternoon? You know the one I mean."

"I know the one you mean," I said. I knew that just as I had called him then I could call him now. I laughed to myself thinking that Bert would risk standing there exposed.

"Damn it, Tom, *did* you?"

And I had them all there again in the person of Bert Kratz and knew I mustn't force it.

"Well, I certainly didn't know *which* beam," I said.

I could see that he knew now that I still had him. He took a step towards me, his hands coming up higher, his grin wiped out. I balanced automatically and leaned forward, ready to step into him.

Something in my eyes must have warned him. "Yeah," he said, catching himself. We looked at each other for a long moment before he said "Yeah" again. "I told Martha I'd find you here. It's time to get back. Dinner's almost ready and we ought to belt down a couple for the end of the probate."

"Yes," I said.

He went up the steps ahead of me. For an instant, seeing his broad rump at eye level I felt a wild impulse to give the bastard a quick goose just for the hell of it. But that, after all, I knew as I shook with unvoiced laughter, would be an acknowledgment, and an acknowledgment was something Bert Kratz was never going to get from me.

On the landing, I stepped through after him, my hand on the loose doorknob. And then, thinking of that other being down in the darkness under the beam, I leaned in and called out, "Goodbye! Don't think I'm ever coming back." I began pulling the door to, and something made me call out before the latch clicked shut, "Nevertheless, I reserve the right."

Bert had started on ahead of me. Now he turned, something like fear parting his lips. "What the hell are you doing?"

I looked into the pale winter sunlight fading now. "Just saying goodbye to my dead brother down there," I said, walking toward him.

"Don't be a fool, Tom," he said. "You never had a brother."

"Oh, didn't you know? Anyway, he's down there dead for good now."

He laughed nervously and began walking on. "You always were a card, Tom. You sometimes put us in stitches that summer. But for Christ's sake, quit it!"

Looking at him going on without turning I thought that he was the one person I'd ever seen who could waddle like a duck and strut like a peacock at the same time. What a flab ass!

"Sure," I said, catching up with him and feeling ashamed. Now that I knew Grandfather Lloyd had been just another fallible human I should at least have the decency to try and change my feeling about Bert. "You find your shipment in Lakeview?"

"What's that?"

"Your shipment for the store," I said, fighting down the thought that nothing about him would ever attract me.

"Oh, that," he said. "Yeah, I finally caught up with it. Those railway boys keep fucking up all the time."

13 &

As we walked north to the house I felt the wind's bite. "That cold front with the snow is moving down fast," I said.

"Sure thing," Bert said, opening the door and stepping aside. As I passed him, saying "Thanks, Bert," I noticed how carefully he avoided looking at me and I thought he must think that I was still a little out of my head.

The warmth of the house and the smell of the roast engulfed us. Martha was there too quickly, asking, "Are you there, Tom, are you all right?"

"Never better," I said, "but it's getting colder fast."

"Bert said he knew where to find you." I saw that she had been afraid.

"Yes, he certainly did," I said as we went into the living room.

Bert came back with our drinks.

"Ah, that's what we all need," Martha said. I still couldn't think of Bert with anything like affection, but I told myself this was just a lingering remainder of everything I'd sloughed off.

"I certainly see things more clearly now," I said. "That summer I didn't see much at all most of the time."

"How could you?" Martha said. "Everyone said you mustn't know, you shouldn't know, you were too young, too delicate, you would be shattered."

"But you did know all the time, damn it, you did know, didn't you?" Bert insisted.

"Not all the details, at least—not even all the details now."

"It took me a long time to believe it myself," Martha said. "It was the *mannerly* part of it, I suppose."

"What a word to use!" I said, remembering Grandma Tessy with her powdered cleavage and her southern speech.

"But it's the right one," she said. "Old Dr. Chapman said to me once that the real trouble with Grandfather Lloyd was the way his wives treated him—*our* grandmother from New England and Grandma Tessy from the South."

"I know," I said, smiling, thinking how much she reminded me of Fran.

"No, I don't think you do," Martha said. "I mean that of course you know about who they were and where they came from, but you don't know what old Dr. Chapman said to me. He said, 'Martha, your Grandfather Lloyd's first wife *moralled* him to death and his second wife *mannered* him to death!'"

Bert snorted and I took a long pull of my drink.

"That's why I used *mannerly,*" Martha said. "Did anyone tell you he asked permission?"

I shook my head.

"Well, he did," she said. "Imagine him going to Tessy and telling her that now Floss was dead and the bank wouldn't come back even after we used every red cent of family money to pay off a hundred cents on the dollar, he didn't care, he didn't want to live, so if she was agreeable he would handle things in his own way."

"And what did she say?"

"Tessy? Oh, all the grand Virginia lady came out. 'Mr. Lloyd, you are not considering *me!*' and all that sort of thing. But he *had* considered her, hadn't he, just by asking? And somehow she had her own money. At least that's what Mom has always insisted. So they took away his razors and guns. Dad and Uncle Drew went everywhere with him. It *was* mannerly, wasn't it? That was the Maryland in him, that half-way life, caught between the north and the south."

I nodded.

"No one paid any mind after a while because someone always stayed with him. But whenever he passed the barn or a stable and saw a bit of rope or heavy twine he picked it up as if he wasn't thinking about it. Then when they'd go down to the bank to work

on the books he'd open the cellar door and toss in his little collection
as if he were tidying up everything."

She took a long breath. I waited. "And that afternoon, when no
one was noticing much because it had been ten days or so since he'd
spoken to Tessy, he just stepped out of the bank 'for a breath of air'
and went around to the side and bolted the door. He tied everything
together carefully, all the bits of rope and cord and a section of
harness strap and when he had finished he stood on a saw horse and
kicked it out from under himself."

We sat there for a while and Bert poured me another drink while
Martha went to see to the roast.

"I didn't know all that," I said to Bert, trying to be generous.

"Well, that's the way it was," he said. I still felt something
between us.

Martha came back and as the three of us walked to the kitchen I
said, "I've never known too much about it. Fact is, I always resented
Grandfather Lloyd, though I couldn't remember him. You know
how everyone talked as if he was a good deal wiser than Solomon."

Before we sat down Martha handed me a sheet of paper, saying,
"Here's the message to Grandma Tessy that was found in one of his
vest pockets, carefully folded and put into an unsealed envelope."

It was a sheet of the bank's bond stationery:

COMMERCIAL BANK OF DALTON

THOMAS D. LLOYD, PRESIDENT

DREW E. LLOYD, CASHIER

DALTON, IOWA

My Dear Tessy

I am worried to death and I fear I shall be a crazy man—
I have worried so much about conditions in general—I fear
this whole America will be a second Russia—How can men
pay when they cannot get the money—How can men work
when there is no work—There never was such a time in the
history of our country it looks as tho the world is bankrupt.

I have worried myself sick about you and Netty—May God
bless you and keep you is my prayer.

Your own Tom

Standing there, I read it again and again until the words had
burned into my memory.

Both Martha and Bert had waited for me to sit down. I handed
the sheet to Martha as I pulled out my chair.

"Russia!" I exclaimed. "You know, I was still fighting the Kaiser
that summer."

Martha smiled as Bert began to carve. "As to Grandfather's
wisdom, I guess the family felt it should say something. But it was
more than that, too," she said.

"Could you tell me about Aunt Floss and the way she died?" I
asked as we started to eat. "Mother always felt that had a great deal to
do with what happened."

"The baby—Kenny—came early. Grandfather hadn't seen her
since she and Kenny's father had had to get married, but I think that
was more her choice than his. Everything went wrong with the
birth. When they couldn't stop the internal bleeding and she knew
she was dying up there in Center City Hospital, she sent word for
him, just him, please to come. She told the doctors she knew she was
going, but for God's sake, to do everything they could to keep her
conscious until he got there. He drove alone in the Liberty Six. She
lasted about twenty minutes after he got there. No one ever knew—
not even Tessy—what they said to each other. It wasn't just the
bank, you know, it wasn't just that he'd been too generous with his
neighbors and now they blamed him for it—it was all that and Floss
and everything—even your mother's going off to China and Drew's
flunking out of college years before."

"Poor devil!" I said.

"What do you mean?" Bert asked.

"Just that he was like all the rest of us," I said. "And all my life I've
resented the way . . . "

"What do you mean like the rest of us?" Bert asked. "Why, you don't know a damn thing about him. You just said you can't even remember seeing him."

"No, I can't," I said. "I don't need to anymore."

"Well, if you could remember him you wouldn't say he was like the rest of us," Bert insisted. I saw Martha glance from him to me and barely shake her head warningly as she caught my eye.

"I remember *your* father, Bert," I said. "He always treated me generously." I thought of the nickel.

Bert wasn't listening. "Yeah, there was a difference between him and the rest. There was a difference all right, and maybe I hated it sometimes—Brooks could be a real snot—and maybe sometimes I thought I could take care of it."

"Of course you could, Bert," I said.

"Even when the bank was getting into trouble I knew there was still a difference."

I wondered why, now that I saw Grandfather Lloyd so human, so suffering and torn and broken, I still couldn't quite deal with this self-satisfied fool. We ate on in silence.

"I whipped up a chocolate cake while you were out, Tom," Martha said, getting up and beginning to clear the table. "How about a slice with some coffee in the living room?"

"That would be wonderful," I said, knowing she was clawing off from everything we had touched on.

When she came into the living room with a tray she said, "You can feel the cold seeping in from the service porch. This front is really going to turn into something!"

Whether she had meant it to be a signal I couldn't tell, and I didn't care, because I knew that for me it was the perfect signal. I had seen the Wyoming acreage. I had come to Dalton and I had dealt with Dalton. True, Bert remained, but I suspected I'd need a long time to fit Bert somehow into my own renewed and freshened life. I felt alive, eager to get back to Amy and the girls, back into the action of my Leaf Out life.

I said, "That front must be coming down faster than anyone thought. I know it may sound impolite to say it, Martha, but I honestly think that after another cup of coffee I'd better put everything in my bag and head south—get ahead of the front and drive as far as I can tonight, even making the first swing west if I can beat it by that much."

"It's an awfully late hour for starting out," Martha said, but I heard no pressure behind her protest.

Bert was close to the point of encouraging me when he said, "There's a chance of your being caught here, I suppose." I saw him looking at Martha, who looked away.

"It's the only sensible thing for me to do," I said. "You don't want to be snowed in for a week with your Chinese cousin, and your Chinese cousin needs to get back to his family and job as fast as he can, anyway. It's really been great, even if it has been so short—great to see you both, see Dalton, see what you've done with the old house."

I knew Bert was relieved. For Martha I couldn't say. She had clearly hoped Aunt Netty and Uncle Carl would come down for the night. With me alone it could be something else again. Maybe she enjoyed encouraging Bert in his delusion—or at least what I took to be his delusion—that by marrying into the Lloyds he had achieved something significant. Certainly Amy, I thought gratefully, would never feel that way.

I didn't take long to pack after I'd changed into my brown checked flannel shirt, thinking of the cold night. I began to feel the pleasure of starting on a trip. And this time I would be starting in the right direction. I'd be properly heading west, coming into a fresh inheritance now that the old illusive one had been settled.

As I carried my bag and briefcase downstairs I saw the two of them standing there. Bert, looking flustered, held a brown paper bag. "Martha said she'd found an almost empty fifth of Teacher's scotch in your room. I picked this up in Lakeview before I came back. Give you a small start."

"Say, that's great," I said. "And how thoughtful of you, Martha." I knew my heart should open to Bert, but it remained stubbornly closed.

We went down the shadowed walk between the walnut trees and

stopped in an awkward pause by the Chevy. Martha and I kissed and promised to keep in touch, knowing we wouldn't, except for a Christmas card each December. Bert handed me the Teacher's, which I put in next to my briefcase, and we shook hands.

"Please don't wait here in the cold without your coats," I said. "It'll take a few minutes to warm up the engine."

They left after the mildest protest, and I waved as they stood in the lighted doorway for an instant before going back into the house. I hadn't so much wanted them to leave as I'd wanted to sit there alone once the engine was turning over. I wanted to look at the house, the lighted windows, the walk, the tall black trees, because I had no intention of ever returning to Dalton.

At last I switched on the headlights, put the car in gear and started off. When I got to the end of Main Street I turned north instead of south and speeded up until I came to the Lakeview road.

I wondered if I had headed for Lakeview because of the shadows on the walk or if this had always been part of my unspoken plan from the beginning. It didn't make any difference either way. Here I was, switching on the radio and turning the dial to pick up some news of the weather. If it had seemed intolerable to be snowed in in Dalton it would be almost as bad to be caught in Lakeview.

We'd been to Lakeview once that summer. I remembered the moldy smell of the bath house where everyone changed in cubicles. But what I remembered most vividly was stepping into the water of the lake and my shock at finding my feet sinking into mud. I'd been used to the white sand beaches of the north China coast. I felt something almost indecent, too stickily physical, about the mud oozing up between my toes.

Certainly there had been no neon lights then, and as I came into the town I saw that Bert was right. Dalton formed part of a dying past, but Lakeview was a coming place. What looked like a couple of nightspots cast streaming red and green and blue reflections over the water from their signs.

I drove into a filling station to gas up. While the attendant worked on the car I went to the phone booth and checked out the name I was hunting for. I memorized the address, and going into the station itself I found a plat of Lakeview tacked on the wall behind a desk. I looked for the street and found it, five blocks back from the waterfront.

"I help you find something?" the attendant asked as he came in and I handed him my credit card.

"No, but thanks very much," I said. "I've already found the place I was looking for on the map."

"I just thought that being from California you might not know your way around," he said.

"I don't, really."

"There are two or three pretty good motels," he offered.

"I'm not staying over," I said. "I've got to head back before that storm comes down."

"Then you'd better hurry," he said. "Last I heard, it was moving faster than they'd thought in the beginning. Sounds like a real humdinger."

That was a word out of the past, I thought. "I reckon," I said.

"You know someone in Lakeview?" he asked. "You been here before?"

"Once, a long time ago when I was a kid I spent a summer in Dalton and we came over here for a swim."

I signed the slip and as we walked to the car I could tell he was trying to place me, guess my age. "You must see a lot of changes."

"There wasn't any neon then and I wasn't old enough to visit any speakeasies." That should help him.

"Dalton," he said. "I guess Dalton used to have a good bit of life in it. Funny place to spend a summer, I'd think."

"We were visiting my mother's family. My grandfather had died and it was a kind of gathering of the clan."

"You came all the way from California for that?"

"I didn't live in California then," I said. "My mother and sister and I came from China."

"China?" he said. "Hell, that's a new one on me! I thought I knew the names of all the small towns in the state."

I saw that I should have said "Shanghai." It was too late now. I smiled at the thought that perhaps I really had an American home town after all: China, Iowa. So I said, "They really hit on some pretty fancy names for a lot of little places, didn't they?"

"I'll say," he said, "and a lot of them never got farther than being much more than a crossroads."

"Right," I said and nodded as I drove out of the station.

I stopped in front of a two-story apartment house and found the name on the mailbox for 203. I couldn't find any bell to ring. Security couldn't be a problem yet in Lakeview. I climbed the stairs and pushed the electric buzzer by the door of 203 and stepped back.

I was on the point of trying the buzzer again when the spy window opened. All I could see was a blur of features, the hallway light catching a pair of blue eyes.

"Miss Heidi Hauser?" I asked.

"Sure, but . . . " she began and stopped.

"I know you won't recognize me," I said quickly, "and I know it's a strange hour to call without warning. But we met—we knew each other—one summer, years ago in Dalton, and I wanted . . . "

"Wait!" she said. "Don't say another word. I can't quite remember you yet, but I will. You said Dalton, didn't you, you have a connection with Dalton?"

"Yes, I . . . "

"No, stop!" she said, unlocking the door. "Just come in and don't say anything, don't tell me your name until I've had a good look at you. Dalton!"

She buttoned the top of her housecoat as she crossed the room and turned down the radio. "Just sit down, and in a minute I'll remember who you are." Her voice held something coquettish in it, something both flirtatious and challenging.

"Really, I can't believe . . . " I began.

She stopped me again with an uplifted hand and I sat down on one end of a sofa. She crossed the room and sat on the other end, tucking her feet under her and looking at me.

"Of course if it has anything to do with Dalton and all that, you're some kind of Lloyd," she said. "I can see that when you smile."

"Well, part Lloyd, anyway," I said.

"No, don't talk," she said, "or maybe you should, after all, because there's something about your voice—and *it's* no part of Dalton—that comes back a little."

"I can't believe you'll recognize me," I said, "though I'm sure you'll remember me once you know. Frankly, I'm a lot better looking now than when I was a kid that summer. And I'm not sure I'd have recognized you, so far as that goes, though I can see a little of your mother in you now that I think of it."

"Of course you're part Lloyd, anyone can see that," she said. "But that voice, that accent. Yes, I've got it! You're Emma Lloyd's son, aren't you? You're the skinny little kid from China!"

"Right," I said, surprised. "That's me all right, the skinny little kid from China."

"Tom," she said. "Wait, I'll get it all—Tom, Tom—I know, Chinky Tom *Jerome!*"

"I'm amazed," I said. "It's incredible that you can bring that back."

"But what are you doing in Lakeview?" she asked. "And why did you think of me? And how did you know where to find me?" She laughed. "That's too much to answer all at once, isn't it? Look, I'll make some coffee—or better, you might like a drink."

"Great," I said.

"Come on out to the kitchen, even if it is a mess. If Mother was alive—she died about four years ago—she'd really lay into me for it."

She had got up and I followed her. The kitchen wasn't all that messy. A drain rack held a couple of tumblers turned upside down, a few dishes, and some silverware. I saw a pair of bottles—one scotch, one bourbon—at the end of the counter. Heidi reached for glasses from a shelf. "Scotch?" she asked and I nodded. She picked up the bottle of Red Label. "Say when."

"Not too much," I said. "There, that's fine. I've got to drive tonight."

"The only water's from the tap," she said, "unless you want ice."

"I'll sip it neat," I said.

Still holding the bottle, she poured a good slug for herself, filled the rest of the glass from the tap, and we went back to the sofa.

"To answer at least one of your questions" I said, "I've been to Dalton to settle Grandfather Lloyd's estate after all these years. I don't know if you ever heard the family talk about some property he'd owned in Wyoming."

"The Wyoming acreage! How could you be around the Lloyds very long without hearing about *that?*"

"I guess everyone did carry on about it."

"On and on," she said. "It was going to be the salvation of the Lloyds after what happened to the bank."

"Well, it's sold now," I said. "I brought some papers my mother had to sign and I've been in Dalton with my cousin Martha whom you may remember. She married Bert Kratz."

"I remember," she said.

"I've been thinking a lot about that summer," I said.

"I feel as if I remember every summer in Dalton and every winter, too."

"I didn't mean quite that," I said. "Just that particular one."

"Of course," she said. "The bank had closed and old Mr. Lloyd had—well, he was dead. And then you and your sister arrived from China and I knew why your hair was so dark."

"And straight," I said.

"Yes, and straight."

"I'm on my way back home now," I said, "but all the time I was on my way from California to Dalton—I guess I haven't said I live in California now—I kept thinking about that summer, the things I learned, the things I didn't understand at first, how everything kept changing. And I thought of you several times."

"Of me?"

"Yes, of you."

"That's nice, I suppose," she said, "but I wasn't anything to you."

"Oh, but you were," I answered. "That's why I'm here tonight. I feel guilty about that summer—about you and that summer."

"I don't get it," she said.

"Maybe you remember the way your mother scrubbed the cement walk with lye to get my sister Fran and me out of trouble."

She looked indifferent. "Really? No, I don't remember that."

"Well, we owed her a lot."

"As I said, Mother died a few years ago."

"Yes, and I'm sorry . . ."

"I wasn't sorry," she broke in. "This is a long way from a made-over caboose."

I hadn't really taken in the apartment. It had a kind of mail-order correctness about it, I felt, glancing around the room.

"Yes, this is nice," I said. "But the reason I felt—I feel—so bad about all that is the way—is what I said to you one time. You know, you were the one person I could pick on, and I was rotten, absolutely rotten."

"Why, you were just a skinny little kid from China who talked in a funny way," she said. "How could *you* have picked on *me?*"

"Maybe you remember how I finally committed the unforgivable sin—betraying the boys' plot—really Bert's plot—to capture Martha and tie her up in the barn."

"Yes," she said flatly. "That was when Bert decided he had a chance, wasn't it? I mean, Martha really wouldn't have minded, would she?"

"No, but I was too young and scared to know that. And it was after that, and a good bit after your mother had bailed us out of the walnut mess that I found out Bert knew I'd peached on him. And later than that, you laughed at me in front of everybody and I turned on you and said—you remember the stupid feeling about Germans still—I said no one wanted to have anything to do with you and you could go back to the Kaiser, the Kaiserin, and all the little Kaiserettes. God, how those stupid, cruel words have stuck in my memory!"

"You said that?" She was a study in coolness, control.

"Don't you remember?" And I saw her eyes now, and I saw them again as she reached out to Bert, the flash of tears, the turning away.

No tears showed. She lifted her glass slowly and sipped at the scotch. "No, I don't remember that at all, Tom." I watched her throat working.

I wanted to tell her she was lying. Then I asked myself what business of mine it was if she wouldn't admit to the memory, the hurt, so I said, "Even if you don't remember, I want to apologize, to say what a stinking thing it was, and that it was only because I was so scared myself that I said it."

"You want to apologize for something so unimportant I can't even remember it?" Again I watched her throat working.

"Yes," I said. "I hope you'll accept it. It would make me feel better."

She looked at me steadily. She took a deep breath. "Of course, Tom, if that's the way you feel. Truly, all I can remember is what a skinny kid you were and how you talked. But it's a long time and a long way from Dalton now."

"That's the truth."

"It is, isn't it? And nobody has to take anything from the Lloyds," she said.

"Well, the Lloyds haven't much to be taken from or to give," I said, "if they ever really did have. Not even the Wyoming acreage."

She relaxed, slumping back against the cushioned back of the sofa. "Yes, that's true," she said, almost as if she had just discovered something. For a moment I thought she was going to go on, but she didn't. She just looked at me and the hint of a smile softened her mouth. "Yes, that's true," she repeated.

So there was nothing more to be said.

"I'm starting back tonight. You know there's a big storm coming down and I don't want to get caught in it. I'll head straight south to beat it."

"Yes," she said, but she wasn't hearing me. She looked beyond me, her eyes unfocused.

Only when I stood did she recover herself, and then, jumping up too quickly and paying no attention to the glass in her hand she moved toward me and splashed some of the scotch onto my shirt front.

"Oh, how stupid of me, how clumsy!"

"It's nothing," I said.

"Here, come into the kitchen, and I'll clean you up."

"No, no, don't bother," I said. "I'll just use your bathroom, if you don't mind, and wash up a bit and then I'll be ready to go."

"Oh dear," she said, as I stepped into what I knew must be the bedroom. She followed in a moment, saying, "At least here's a clean towel."

When I came back to the living room she was still standing. I took her hand and said, "Well, goodbye, Heidi. I'm glad I found you to apologize, because I don't plan ever to come back to Dalton or Lakeview."

Something of her early flirtatiousness had returned. "I did get your name at last, didn't I? I'll bet you were surprised."

"I *was*," I said.

Outside and starting up the Chevy, I knew I was really on my way home. I had no more stops to make. I would run south in front of the storm and later, somewhere in Kansas, in Missouri if I had to, I'd start the swing west. Back to where I belonged, back to Amy and Mary and Maude and my own freshly inventive Leaf Out life that looked more than ever inviting to me now.

I couldn't think that I would ever completely forget Dalton or the Wyoming acreage or Mrs. Hauser's red hands or the beam in the cellar of the bank. But if those memories blurred and shifted, as they probably would, I knew I would never forget the look of the churned-up bedclothes there in Heidi Hauser's apartment and the creased wine-colored pajamas with the blue piping that hung on the hook screwed into the back of the bathroom door.